"Is this what you want?" he whispered

His head moved slowly downward and she froze, dumbly staring at his mouth, hypnotized by the male curve of it as it came closer. Jake's hand moved slowly up her arm, over her bare shoulder to her throat. His lips warmly touched her mouth and Sasha felt her own lips part, heard her heart begin to beat heavily as a melting heat flowed inside her.

She thought she had absorbed all the pain long ago, but it had only been forced down inside of her, a frozen block of anguish that had never thawed. It was melting now, in the heat of her own desire and Jake's passionate caresses. She felt it bursting up out of her, hurting her throat; hard, deep cries of grief that left her raw....

Books by Charlotte Lamb

These books may be available at your local bookseller.

For a free catalog listing all titles currently available,
send your name and address to:

Harlequin Reader Service
P.O. Box 52040, Phoenix, AZ   85072-9988
Canadian address: Stratford, Ontario   N5A 6W2

CHARLOTTE LAMB

a secret intimacy

Harlequin Books

TORONTO • NEW YORK • LONDON
AMSTERDAM • PARIS • SYDNEY • HAMBURG
STOCKHOLM • ATHENS • TOKYO • MILAN

Harlequin Presents first edition January 1984
ISBN 0-373-10658-0

Original hardcover edition published in 1983
by Mills & Boon Limited

CHAPTER ONE

SASHA slid her tightly fitting dress down over her hips and stepped out of it with a sigh of relief; the red velvet was far too hot on a night like this, but when the costumes were designed it had been midwinter and nobody had expected the play to run for as long as it had. It was only coming off now because the management had booked a revival of *St Joan* into the theatre months ago and could not find another theatre to switch either play to at such short notice. She could hear some of the cast walking past, talking excitedly, high on the euphoria of the last-night curtain calls. She felt rather melancholy, herself; this had been her first West End run, who knew when she would get another chance? She was going to miss the friends she had made during these months and she wasn't looking forward to the hassle of auditions and visits to agents.

'Hot out front tonight, wasn't it?' Maggie murmured, and Sasha turned to look across their shared dressing-room, feeling too deliciously cool in her bra and panties to bother to put on her robe.

'Like an oven; I could hear people fanning themselves all over the house,' she agreed.

Maggie looked at her reflection with distaste. 'God, I look like a decomposing prune—I knew this make-up was too heavy, my skin will never be the same again. I'm turning old right in front of my eyes!'

Sasha laughed, lifting her black hair from her perspiring neck. 'You look fine to me!'

Maggie was eyeing her in the dressing-table mirror, her thin brows expressive. 'You're horribly thin—haven't got anorexia, have you?'

'I wish I had,' said Sasha ruefully, surveying her own reflection from behind Maggie's shoulder-blades without much satisfaction. The proportions of her body were all wrong: she was badly designed, she had often felt, her waist and hips too slender, her breasts too full and her legs far too long. 'It would help if I didn't get too hungry over the next few weeks—God knows when I'll get another job, my agent hid in a cupboard when I went to his office yesterday and his receptionist was ominously sympathetic as she assured me she would be in touch soon. I've saved quite a bit out of my salary from this run, but most of that will have to go on rent.'

'Something will turn up,' Maggie said optimistically. 'You had very good notices.'

'Two,' Sasha said. 'The *Daily Mail* said I had good legs and one of the *Times* reviews mentioned me as being among the cast.'

'At least they didn't ignore you,' said Maggie, looking on the bright side; she didn't need to worry about where the next job was coming from, she had a husband in full-time employment outside the theatre, not to mention a whole army of friends inside it who could put in a good word for her when casting was being done. All Sasha had was a far from understanding bank manager who was only prepared to extend her overdaft after he had chased her around his desk until he collapsed into his chair purple with excitement.

'I'll probably have to work in my brother's shop for a while,' Sasha decided aloud, considering herself in the mirror again. The dressing-room was tiny, barely more than a cupboard, and there wasn't room for more than one of them at the dressing-table, they had to take turns in front of the mirror. She was still wearing her stage make-up; her eyes darkly outlined, lids gleaming blue above the darker blue of the iris. Her features were fine-boned, ultra-sensitive; her cheeks slightly hollowed below the high angle of the bone, her nose apparently designed to be long and slender but with a sudden tilt at the tip which left the impression of wicked impertinence when she smiled, her skin beneath the heavy stage make-up smooth and flawless, her mouth generous, passionate, widely modelled. It was an unusual face and certainly not a beautiful one, but Sasha could convey the image of beauty when she went out of her way to do so, when she was lit up men looked twice; but without make-up and in a dull mood she was very ordinary.

'I shan't be a second,' said Maggie, removing the last trace of blusher from her cheeks. She was a Leo, with yellow lion's eyes and a magnetic personality; although she usually drawled in a lazy way she could roar like a lion if you crossed her. Sasha had learnt to be wary of her temper during the past two months of their run. Maggie was easy-going and goodhumoured most of the time, but when she did fly into a rage everyone in earshot took cover. She was an experienced, highly regarded actress who would never be a star but was usually in work. Sasha had been very nervous of sharing a dressing-room with her at first; it wasn't easy for a comparative newcomer to live cheek by jowl with such an established actress, but Maggie was generous and friendly, Sasha felt she had learnt more from her in a few weeks than she had in months at her drama school.

'Looking forward to the party? What are you wearing?' Maggie asked as she got up from the stool.

'My new blue dress,' said Sasha, standing sideways to allow Maggie to pass in the constricted room, and at that moment someone tapped at the door and without waiting for an invitation came into the room.

Maggie turned quickly, her eyes bright with rage which vanished as she looked at the slim young woman standing smiling at her. Sasha had never seen her before, but Maggie's face lit up. 'Caro! Where did you spring from? Were you out front tonight? I didn't even notice you, why didn't you come round in the interval or wave a paw—where were you sitting?'

'Third row,' the other woman told her. She was very attractive, closer to Maggie's age than to Sasha's; her red-gold hair worn in a loose cluster of curls and her face expertly made up. She could have been an actress, but whatever she did she was very successful at it, Sasha guessed, because the black velvet suit she was wearing was too elegant and beautifully cut to have been bought in a department store, it must have cost the earth. 'You were terrific, Maggie, we loved every minute of it—what a pity it has to come off. The house was very full tonight, I'm sure it could have run much longer.'

'Tell the management,' Maggie said drily, then

in a different tone: 'You said we? Is James with you?'

'No,' the other woman said, her lips wry, and Sasha glanced curiously from one to the other of them, picking up some nuance in the conversation which she could not quite pin down. Someone shifted behind the redheaded woman and Sasha suddenly realised there was a man standing just on the threshold. Maggie hadn't noticed him yet, but Sasha began to inch her way towards the towelling robe hanging on a hook on the wall. She was only wearing bra and panties, she wasn't dressed for receiving visitors. Over Maggie's shoulder she met a pair of vivid blue eyes set beneath thick black brows which lifted in silently mocking appraisal for a second before Sasha could slide out of his line of vision and hurriedly shrug herself into the robe.

It had all happened too fast for her to do more than take in a vague impression of him, but even as she was tying the belt of the robe she was frowning, trying to remember where she had seen him before. The face had been familiar—hadn't it? Maggie had seen him at last, she was brimming with excitement, her voice rising.

'Jake! I don't believe it! I thought you were in the States, when did you get back? Is the film finished? God, you look brown, you didn't get that out of a bottle!'

'Hallo, Maggie darling,' said a deep, dark brown voice which held laughter and an audible affection.

'He only flew in yesterday, he says the film's a stinker,' the other woman said. 'He does look well, doesn't he? They were on location in Mexico, Jake spent most of the time sunbathing.'

'Or serenading the local señoritas,' Maggie said tartly, and both women laughed as though the man standing between them was not present and couldn't hear what they were saying about him. Sasha was standing well back, listening and trying to remember where she had heard that film, seen that face before—it must have been in a film, she decided. There could be only one Jake in Maggie's life, she had talked about him non-stop over the past two months, she was very proud of her friendship with one of the cinema's leading stars and quite shocked when Sasha admitted she hadn't seen any of his films. Sasha suffered from migraine, she never went to the cinema because it made her eyes blur to sit in the dark and watch an image on a screen, and by some chance she had never caught any of Jake Redway's films on television. She had been far too busy over the past four years to watch television except on an occasional, desultory basis. All the same, both face and voice had run bells inside her head. Maybe she had seen one of his films some time, and forgotten it.

'How's Madeleine?' asked Maggie, and the woman she called Caro laughed.

'She's fine. She'll be two next month, isn't that amazing?'

'Amazing,' mocked Jake Redway. 'We do all get older, though, hadn't you noticed?'

She turned her bright head to look at him, and Sasha sensed intimacy between them, an easy understanding. 'She's got so much energy now that she can get about on her own two feet. By the time she goes to bed I'm worn out!'

'Who's babysitting tonight?' asked Maggie, and again there was that dryness in her voice. 'James?' Somehow the way she pronounced the name told you that she expected the answer to be no; but Caro gave her a long look and nodded.

'He loves it when I go out and leave her with him—he worships the ground she walks on.'

'Well, he's a very possessive man,' Jake Redway drawled, and Sasha saw Caro frown, her slanting green eyes troubled.

'You must both come to our party,' Maggie told them, linking an arm with each and looking from one to the other, face satisfied. 'We're having it at the Connaught—you'll come, won't you? You aren't driving home tonight, Caro?'

'No, I'm staying in London, I'm at a hotel. I had to come up to have some tests at the London hospital.'

'What sort of tests? What's wrong?' Maggie asked, immediately anxious, and Caro squeezed her arm, looking at her with reassuring warmth.

'Nothing serious. My own doctor thinks I'm anaemic, he wants to make sure there's nothing much wrong—I had a couple of fainting spells, but I'm sure it was just because I was on a very strict diet.'

'What on earth do you need to diet for?' asked Jake, roughness in his tone. 'You're too skinny already.'

Sasha saw Maggie exchange a glance with him, their expressions identical: uneasy, concerned, worried. She wished Jake Redway and Caro would leave so that she could take off her make-up and change for the party. There was something about the way they talked to each other which made her feel excluded. None of them were so much as looking in her direction, she might as well have been a fly on the wall. She was not of their clan, and that apparently made her invisible. Sasha did not like that, she felt awkward hovering on the outside of their tight little circle. She stared at them, willing them to go, and Jake Redway's eyes met hers again.

She had the same odd sense of *déjà vu*—where had she seen him before? It could have been anywhere, of course—he was famous, his face was always in front of the public, she could have passed over pictures of him in newspapers or on TV without fitting the name to the face.

Maggie looked round, threw her an apologetic smile. 'Oh, Sasha, I'm sorry, come and meet Jake and Caro. This is Sasha Lewis, she played . . .'

'We noticed,' Jake Redway drawled. 'You did the part very well.'

Caro held out her hand, smiling. She was rather pale, tiny beads of sweat on her forehead, and as they shook hands Sasha asked anxiously: 'Are you okay?' There was something fragile about the other woman, the vivid blaze of her red-gold hair and her obvious vivacity were in opposition to the delicacy of her features and her slender body. Sasha could understand why Maggie and Jake Redway treated her as though she was made of fine porcelain.

Caro forced a laugh. 'It's so hot in here, how can you bear it?'

'You're not going to faint!' Jake exclaimed, and looked round the room. A chipped jug of water stood on the dressing-table, they had been sipping water during the interval. Maggie rushed to find a glass and held it, Jake poured water into it while Caro sat down on the stool, all the colour draining out of her face.

'Sorry,' she said, and Maggie looked impatient. Sasha crouched down beside her and rubbed her chilly hands. Jake took the glass from Maggie and leaned over to put the rim of it to Caro's lips, and Sasha looked up at him and saw his face at an odd angle. It looked very different now: he was frowning, his skin pale, his black brows a heavy line across his forehead. She saw him in close detail; the graining of the skin magnified as he lifted the glass and the contents tilted sideways showing Sasha his face through the water. It was at that instant that she remembered him, knew where she had seen him before—and her mind froze, her body froze with it, the tiny incident releasing a deeply buried memory which made her rigid with pain.

Caro drank, eyes half closed. Jake took away the glass and Maggie put a hand on the back of Caro's neck, pushing her head down between her legs. Sasha hadn't moved, she stayed silent, unaware of everything around her.

'Should we get a doctor?' Maggie asked Jake in a low voice.

'I'll take her back to her hotel,' he said.

'She's never been very strong, sometimes I get so angry . . .' Maggie was whispering, but audibly, and Caro slowly sat up, smiling at her.

'I'm fine now—it was just the heat down here. I'm not going to miss your party, it's years since I was at a last-night party, I wouldn't miss this one for worlds.'

'No,' said Jake Redway. 'I'm taking you back to

your hotel. Don't argue, Caro. You're as white as a sheet.' He lifted her, an arm around her waist and she shrugged ruefully.

'You're as much a bully as James, in your way!'

'Don't compare me with Fox, for God's sake,' Jake muttered.

'Maggie, I'm sorry about the party,' Caro said, ignoring that.

'Forget it, just look after yourself. How do you manage to get yourself into these states? James ought to get someone to help you, you do too much.'

'He offered,' Caro protested quickly. 'In fact, he argued with me for weeks, but I wanted to look after Madeleine myself. If you miss those first few years you never get them back, and I love looking after her.' She gave Maggie a placating smile. 'And I do have a daily woman coming in to look after the house, you know. That much James insisted on . . .'

'You ought to take a long holiday,' Maggie told her. 'Get someone to look after Madeleine and go away on a cruise, you need to rest.'

'And leave Madeleine? How could I? I don't trust anyone with her,' said Caro, her mouth curling in self-derision. 'I'll have to look for someone trustworthy to help me, but they don't grow on trees, you know. I don't want a nanny who'll try to come between me and Madeleine, it has to be someone I like and can trust.'

'You're just being pigheaded,' Maggie told her roughly. 'What do you want? The moon?'

'Come on,' said Jake Redway, frowning over her shoulder at Maggie.

'Are you coming back to the party?' Maggie

asked him, and he shrugged without enthusiasm,
but Caro looked at him quickly and sighed.

'Of course he is—Jake, you will, won't you? I'd
have loved to go, you can tell me all about it.'

'I ought to get some sleep myself,' he said flatly.

Caro glanced at Maggie, whose mouth had
turned down at the edges. Sasha was standing up,
very carefully. She had come back to the present
from the dark past in which she had been briefly
trapped. No wonder she hadn't recognised his
face—she had not wanted to remember him. She
didn't recall ever hearing his name at the time, she
had simply wiped all memory of him out of her
mind. Keeping her eyes averted from him, she
looked instead at Caro, who was smiling at him
pleadingly.

'Don't be difficult, Jake—do go to Maggie's
party!'

'If he doesn't want to . . .' Maggie began
aggressively, and Jake looked at her with wry
amusement.

'Don't start getting sulky—I'll come to your
damned party, take that look off your face.'

'Don't do us any favours,' sniffed Maggie, chin
in the air and her growling voice in use.

'The Connaught, you said? I'll be back when
I've dropped Caro off at her hotel.'

Caro held out her hand to Sasha. 'Sorry about
all the fuss, I'd love to have talked to you, I
thought you were wonderful, I'm quite sure I'm
going to be seeing you in much bigger parts soon.'

'Thank you,' Sasha said with an effort; her voice
felt dry, the words seemed to rustle in the air like
dead leaves.

'She's waiting for offers,' Maggie said drily. 'No

luck so far, but they'll come one day; she's too good to go unnoticed.'

'And in the meantime I'm appearing as a shop assistant in what I hope will be a very short run,' Sasha said with a flash of angry humour. Caro looked at her, eyes sympathetic, and Sasha added: 'Luckily for me my brother has an antique shop and will always give me a part-time job when I'm desperate.'

Jake said: 'Come on, Caro! Stop chatting.'

' 'Bye, Maggie, see you again soon . . .'

They went out, closing the door, and Sasha sank down on to the dressing-table stool to stare at herself in the mirror. At close quarters her make-up was twopence coloured, as gaudy as a fairground, but under it her skin was dead white and her blue eyes were dilated, brilliant with remembered pain, the dark centres enormous. She dragged the curling black strands of her hair back and pinned them on top of her head while she cleaned her face.

'I wonder if he will come,' Maggie muttered, reaching down the glittering black dress she meant to wear.

Sasha had removed every trace of make-up, her skin shone in the harsh lights. She hoped desperately that Jake Redway would not come on to the party, she could not bear to see him again now that she knew who he was, she wouldn't be able to see him without remembering. He hadn't recognised her, obviously, but then why should he? It would not have meant much to him, a brief unpleasant incident, no more.

'It changes them, you know,' said Maggie, stepping into her dress and wriggling herself into the tight tube. She was very thin; but she had whipcord strength, she never tired even after twelve hours' rehearsal. Sasha had been awed by her stamina. 'Zip me up, would you?' Maggie asked, and Sasha stood up to do so then stepped aside so that Maggie could get to the mirror to renew her make-up.

'I know he's a big star these days. I suppose our party is small beer to him after the jetsetting parties he usually goes to—but he forgets. This is where it's at, on a stage in front of a live audience, that's what acting is really all about. Did you see that last film he made? I winced. Sheer, unadulterated phoney rubbish! I suppose he did it for the money, but you can't call that acting.'

Sasha had taken off her robe and was getting into her dress, only half her attention on what Maggie was saying in that aggressive voice.

'It's time he came back to where he belongs and did some real work,' Maggie went on, brushing her black hair vigorously so that sparks flew. 'Before he forgets he's an actor and not a sex symbol.' She put down the brush and stood up to study herself in the mirror, smoothing down her dress. 'How do I look?'

'Fantastic,' Sasha said. She sat down and did her own make-up while Maggie collected her various belongings.

While she was outlining her lips and painting them with pink gloss, she stared at herself fixedly. He hadn't recognised her, there hadn't been a flicker in those vivid blue eyes, she must have changed a great deal since that night. She knew she had, she felt so different. In a sense she had died that night, and when she came back to the real world she was another girl. For a long time she had avoided the memory of what happened, she had been too much of a coward to bear the pain. Why had Jake Redway come here tonight? She did not want to see him again: the last time she saw him she had looked at him with bitter hatred, inside her head now she could still hear herself screaming at him, yelling hoarsely until he hit her and everything went black.

'Is Caro an actress?' she asked without turning, and Maggie stood by the door, her mouth wry, hesitating before she answered.

'She trained with us, Jake and me, but she got married and left the theatre.'

'Her husband isn't an actor?'

'He's a barrister, quite well-known—James Fox, have you heard of him?'

Sasha shook her head, getting up, the smooth blue silk of her dress rustling against her thighs. The neckline was very demure, but the skirt was slit at the sides, and when she walked it fell back to reveal her long legs.

'He's a cold bastard,' said Maggie, opening the door. 'I rarely get to see Caro, he won't let he come to London very often.' She paused, frowning. 'I hope there's nothing seriously wrong with her, Caro isn't made of the same stuff as other people. It would break Jake's heart if anything happened to her.' She stopped short, giving Sasha a hurried look, her face flushing. 'We're all very close,' she said quickly, and Sasha thought: but how close? Maggie was famous for putting her foot in it—what had she just blurted out about Jake Redway? Or had she merely phrased the remark badly, given it too much drama? Maggie was famous for that, too; she created drama in everything she did.

They shared a taxi to the hotel at which the party was being held, squeezing into the cab with three others from the cast. Sasha found herself far too close to one of them, an actor in his late forties who was obsessively determined to pretend he was still around thirty, dressed in the very latest fashions and used every opportunity to flirt with her, so heavily that she did not know whether to laugh or show her impatient distaste. She had met his wife several times, and was sorry for her. When Adrian's thigh pressed against her own she shifted along towards Maggie, who looked sideways and winked, guessing at once why Sasha was making herself so thin.

'We wondered if Jake was coming on to the party,' Adrian said across Sasha, his voice loaded with sarcasm. 'But he left, didn't he? He's out of our league now, we're not good enough for him.'

'He had to take Caroline home, he may come on to the party later.' Maggie sounded curt, she was on her dignity.

'I knew I'd seen her before,' said Adrian, sounding triumphant. 'Caroline Fox, wasn't she in that Napoleon series with him?'

'That's right.'

'She's his lady bird, isn't she?' said Adrian, grinning. Sasha found his expression offensive, but then she found almost everything about Adrian rather offensive. He was only jumping to the same conclusion to which she had leapt herself, but there was a salacious amusement in his face which turned her stomach.

'No, she is not,' Maggie retorted, and then,

being Maggie, could contain herself no longer and spat out: 'You've got a disgusting mind, Adrian!'

He merely laughed, as though she was flattering him. Sasha was relieved when the taxi stopped and she coud climb out into the street. Even at this hour the heat was oppressive, there wasn't a breath of air and the sky was a sweltering blue, starless and deep.

The party was a noisy, lively affair with a cold buffet and plenty to drink. The cast and everyone else who had worked on the play was there, many of them had brought husbands or wives, and a number of friends had drifted on from their own performances in other theatres. People moved from group to group, the room gradually so crowded that Sasha found it claustrophobic. Somebody opened a window, sending a little breeze into the room, and she moved towards it, glass in her hand.

'Hallo,' a voice said as she was slipping between two little knots of chattering people, and she looked round, her curly black hair swinging back over her shoulder. It was a reflex action, and even as she made it, she was recognising the voice and stiffening. She stared at him, unsmiling, and could not speak.

Jake Redway's black brows lifted, mocking amusement in his face. 'We met earlier, don't you remember? In Maggie's dressing-room?'

'Yes,' Sasha said, her lips dry as she released the word. They were standing so close she was very conscious of his height. He was much taller than herself, and, as she had good reason to remember, much more powerful: his shoulders broad, his chest deep, his lean body smoothly muscled under the elegant lightweight pale grey suit.

'Unusual name, Sasha,' he commented, putting a hand on her arm and steering her towards the open window. 'Is this what you were making for? Some air?'

'Yes,' she said again, still breathless, trying to think of a way of escaping.

'Is it your real name or a stage name?' He released her arm and put a hand on the wall, propping himself up with a naturally graceful movement which drew attention to the tapering length of his body. He looked as if he meant to stand there all night.

'It's my real name.' She looked out into the street; the traffic sounds came up to her in a distant roar and the lights of London flashed for miles. The city was still wide awake, people were heading out of it after a Saturday night out.

'How long have you been in the business, was this your first West End show?' He was watching her profile, she felt that stare intensely. 'You're good,' he said abruptly before she could answer him. 'It only just shows at the moment, but when you were on I kept looking at you even though you only had a few lines.' He laughed softly. 'And that isn't a line, I mean it. The minute you walked on I felt I knew you. When it happens it usually means . . .' He broke off as she paled, her body rigid. 'What's wrong?'

'I'm so hot,' Sasha said. It was the only excuse she could come up with at the moment. She was feeling sick as she realised that he, too, had felt instant recognition. He might not have worked out yet where he had seen her before, but sooner or later he would, and she dreaded the thought of how he would look at her. She couldn't bear to see that expression in his eyes, she had fought to put the past behind her and she did not want those old wounds reopened.

Jake Redway shot her a look, his black lashes lowered so that only a gleam of those blue eyes showed. She saw his hard mouth curl. 'I know somewhere cool and quiet,' he said, and she heard the proposition in his voice and was instantly angry. He hadn't talked to Caro in that tone, he had a very different voice for her, a million light years from the mocking, self-assured intimacy he was using for Sasha. She knew that sort of attitude, she had met it over and over again in the past few years. Jake Redway took his women lightly, he felt he was doing them a terrific favour by going to bed with them and his ego left no room for an honest relationship; he believed he was giving when he was only taking, meaning to walk away afterwards without looking back, as though each girl was as meaningless and easily forgotten as a take-away Chinese dinner.

She gave him a glacial smile. 'Oh, I'm fine where I am, thanks—I've been looking forward to this party for days.'

'I want to talk to you in private,' he said as if he hadn't caught the icy tone in her voice, and he smiled coaxingly, lazy self-confidence in the blue eyes. 'I've got a proposal to make to you that may interest you.'

Sasha laughed shortly. 'Don't tell me, let me guess—you might consider me to star in your next film?' Her voice cracked like a whip and her face was contemptuous. 'Don't bother to wave that old carrot in front of my nose—I wasn't born yesterday.'

He straightened, his eyes suddenly sharp. 'You've got me wrong.'

'Oh, I don't think so, you're fairly easy to type.'

'Am I, now?' he drawled. The narrowed eyes moved from her flushed and angry face down over her slender but very feminine body in the deceptively demure blue dress. 'I wouldn't say the same about you,' he observed at last, looking back into her eyes. 'I had you down as the quiet mouse in a corner, that's how you were playing it in Maggie's dressing-room—now I'm not so sure. You have a very nasty tongue, Miss Lewis, and an even nastier mind.' Under the coolly delivered words she heard anger, it iced each syllable, and her eyes flickered uncertainly. Had she misinterpreted him after all?

'While I was driving Caro back to her hotel we were discussing you,' he said crisply. 'It occurred to Caro that as you were in need of a temporary job until you got another part you might consider helping her out with her little girl for a few weeks.'

Sasha drew a sharp breath, her face startled. 'Oh . . . I see . . .'

'That,' he said, underlining the words with a straight, hard stare, 'was the proposition I wanted to put to you. A noisy party didn't seem the right place to discuss it.'

'I'm sorry, I got the wrong impression,' she muttered, her eyes falling.

'Yes, didn't you?' he mocked. 'You should watch that—every guy who gives you a smile isn't propositioning you.' He made her sound like an hysterical virgin, dry irony in his voice, and from apologetic embarrassment she flared right back into aggression, her chin going up and her eyes furious.

'If I did make a mistake it was your fault . . .'

'Oh, of course, it would be,' he said, interrupting. Sasha ignored him, finishing her sentence over his words.

'You're so used to investing every word you say with heavy sex appeal that you don't even know you're doing it any more—I bet that even when you ask someone the time you come on like some third-rate Casanova!'

It wasn't until she had stopped talking that she realised that everyone in earshot had been listening to her, the level of conversation had dropped like a stone in their vicinity while the party tuned in to their argument. Sasha glanced round, face hot, and saw amused faces, heard amused whispers and laughter. She looked back at Jake Redway and there was no matching amusement in his face: he looked at her with cold rage, and she had seen that force in his eyes before, she knew it and shrank from it, almost expecting him to hit her, as he had hit her once before.

People began talking again, pointedly, rather more loudly. Under cover of their voices Jake Redway said through tight lips: 'You should have brought your megaphone, some people may not have heard you.'

She turned to push her way through the throng, but he closed iron fingers around her arm and held her there. 'Oh, no, you don't, lady, you aren't walking out on me just yet. That would really give them something to talk about!'

'I'm all out of polite small talk,' Sasha muttered, head bent. He was wearing an after-shave with a clean, cool fragrance, she was so close now that she could see faint darkness along his jaws, infinitesimal black hairs already growing again.

'You're supposed to be an actress,' he told her bitingly. 'So, act.' Anger was emphasising the angularity of his bone structure; he was not a handsome man, his features were too individual and tough for good looks, but their masculinity was pronounced enough to make every woman who saw him very conscious of his sexuality. Sasha slid a sideways look at him as he ran a smoothing hand over his dark hair, his posture casual, as though they were chatting carelessly. Yes, she thought, he was an actor, he was acting at this moment. He looked down at her and smiled dazzlingly, but the smile was only on his lips, his eyes held something very different.

'I'll give you Caro's phone number, you can ring her when you've thought about her suggestion,' he said, and her eyes widened in surprise.

'The job's still on offer, then?' She had expected that he would withdraw the proposal after what had just happened.

He considered her, then insolence came into his face. 'It's Caro who has to put up with you, not me,' he said, and the way he said it made it clear that as far as he was concerned he would be very happy never to set eyes on her again. Sasha stared back at him, willing her eyes to hand him back the same message, and from the hardening brightness of his eyes she knew her silent retort had got home. He let go of her arm and straightened away from her.

'Maggie will have Caro's number,' he said. 'Don't leave it too long, Caro needs help badly.' Then he turned and moved away, and Sasha went in the opposite direction, a phoney smile pinned to her face.

CHAPTER TWO

'SORRY we couldn't make it to your last night,' said Billy, regarding her over the top of his hornrimmed spectacles. 'It was unlucky it clashed with the annual dinner of Karen's luncheon club; she's secretary, she'd organised the whole damned thing and there was no way we could get out of going.'

'Doesn't matter,' said Sasha, perching on a velvet-covered footstall, her jean-clad legs together and her chin resting on her knees.

'How many curtains?'

'Six, but I think Hall dragged it out rather, the audience was half-hearted by the time we got to number six; a lot of them had shoved off.' Behind her she heard a young American talking to a diminutive blonde as they peered at some silver candlesticks. The shop was almost empty, but then it usually was. Sasha could never understand how Billy made it pay. She had asked him once, and he had laughed and tweaked her ear, telling her he could make more profit in one sale a day than he could if he ran a grocery. Billy did not buy junk, he was only interested in really high quality antiques, and he specialised in silver; he was something of an expert on the various silversmiths and their work, particularly of the eighteenth century.

Billy was six years older than Sasha. As a young man he had been very good-looking, his black hair and grey eyes, lean hollowed face, rather poetic; all

26

her friends at school had been madly in love with him, she had never known whether they wanted to know her or Billy. A university student, in jeans and a T-shirt, he had somehow contrived to look Byronic as her friends giggled and nudged each other when they saw him. His grey eyes surveyed them with world-weary cynicism and sent them into delirium. Sasha found it inexplicable: she knew that Billy's remote look came from needing spectacles and being too vain to put them on except in private, and his silence did not indicate higher intelligence, only shyness, but being Billy's sister gave her a status she had never had before, so she held her tongue. When he married Karen, the year he took his degree, the entire sixth form went into aggrieved mourning and Sasha had to put up with an intensive catechism about her new sister-in-law. The only thought which consoled her friends was that this unknown girl must be ravishing, a breathtaking beauty. Sasha discreetly said very little; she had seen Karen. When her friends saw her they were flabbergasted. Short, slightly plump, with warm brown eyes and straight brown hair, Karen was no Helen of Troy. Asked incredulously: but what does he see in her? Sasha could only say lamely: I suppose he loves her.

Eight years later, the same answer applied— Karen and Billy were quietly happy and Billy wore his spectacles all the time, secure in the knowledge that Karen loved him enough to make sure he wore them in case he had an accident. Constant peering at hallmarks which had faded with time had made him even more shortsighted.

'Any hope of a new job yet?' Billy asked, and she made a face, shaking her head.

He smiled at her, the heavy hornrims slipping even further down his nose. 'I can always do with some help in the shop. The girl I have working for me at the moment chews gum all day, I'm terrified she'll start parking it on one of my George III sugar bowls!'

'Thanks, Billy,' said Sasha, smiling back. During her three years' training at drama school she had been very hard-up and Billy had always helped her, and she had learnt a good deal about silver by working in his shop during the holidays. She was about to tell Billy about the suggestion made by Jake Redway when the young American came over, holding one of the candlesticks tentatively. Billy got up, pushing his spectacles back up his nose.

'Nice, aren't they?' It was more than just an opening gambit, Billy was an enthusiast and he loved the antiques he sold. He took the candlestick and his long, thin hands caressed it lovingly, as he began to talk about the man who had made it.

Sasha got up and walked through into the storeroom at the back of the shop. Her sister-in-law was unwrapping the contents of a packing-case and looked round cheerfully.

'I heard your voice—did Billy explain . . .'

'About last night? Yes, forget it, it was hardly an event of national importance. When I open in a starring role I'll expect you both there in the front row, though.'

'Wild horses wouldn't keep us away,' Karen promised, holding up an elegantly chased teapot. 'Look at that, Billy had to pay the earth to get it.' She breathed on the silver and rubbed it with a soft cloth. 'Going to work for us for a while?'

'Well, that's just it,' said Sasha. 'Somebody did offer me a job, but I don't know whether to take it or not.' She told Karen about Jake Redway and Caro, and Karen's round face stretched into a comic mask of fascinated attention; eyes rounding, mouth dropping open.

'Jake Redway? You mean *the* Jake Redway? The film star?'

'That's the guy.' Sasha's voice was short, for some inexplicable reason she resented Karen's excitement about him.

'What's he like in real life? Is he as sexy as . . .'

'He thinks he is,' Sasha broke in, and Karen laughed.

'Oh, conceited, is he? Well,' she added tolerantly, 'I suppose that's to be expected—after all, he is the number one sex object in the States, they say. I enjoy his films, he's got a sense of humour, which is more than you can say about some of them. His eyes smile, don't they?'

Not at me, Sasha thought, remembering the murderous expression in his blue eyes last night.

'How old is this baby?' Karen asked, and Sasha lifted her shoulders in a shrug.

'I don't know, I haven't talked to Caro Fox yet. Maggie gave me her phone number, and I said I'd ring her later this afternoon. She was staying in London last night and driving back home this morning.'

Karen had finished emptying the packing-case. She went over to a sink and washed her hands thoroughly, dried them and turned to consider Sasha with her head to one side; it made her look like a plump little robin, in her cherry-red blouse and brown pleated skirt, one that has heard a worm tunnelling under the grass and is waiting to pounce.

'Well, it's up to you, of course—do you fancy the idea of playing mother's help for a while? You're always wonderful with the boys.' Karen had two sons, the younger five, the elder seven; Sasha could hear them now upstairs in the living-room above the shop, and from the bleeping noises and giggles she guessed they were playing with the video game which Billy had given the seven-year-old, Alex, for his birthday last week.

'Mrs Fox seemed very delicate,' Sasha said irrelevantly, or was it irrelevant? She had only met the woman briefly, yet she had found herself concerned about her ever since, the memory of Caro's mixture of fragility and vivacity kept coming back to her.

Karen frowned. 'That sounds ominous—I know the type, they droop like cut flowers if anyone asks them to lift a hand and you find yourself doing everything.'

'No, she isn't a hypochondriac! She seemed genuine to me.' Sasha frowned, her thoughts confused. 'Maggie's very fond of her,' she said, again with apparent irrelevance, and Karen laughed.

'And you're fond of Maggie?'

'Maggie's nobody's fool,' Sasha tried to explain what she had not yet clarified in her own mind. 'She wouldn't like Caro Fox if she was a phoney.' She smiled at her sister-in-law, her face clearing. 'I liked her too, when she looks at you she sees you, and so many people don't, have you noticed? They look at you and God knows what they're seeing, it isn't you, their eyes never really register you—

maybe all they ever see is themselves, you're just a mirror for them.'

Karen picked up a kettle and filled it at the sink. Turning to plug it into the electric socket, she laughed sideways at Sasha, shaking her head. 'Sometimes you lose me,' she said. 'You take things too seriously—you always did, and it worries me.' Karen did not like the highs and lows of life, she preferred to stay in the shallows, quietly making her way without upheaval. She looked askance at painful emotion, her love for Billy was very close to her love for her two little boys. She mothered all three, she was happy to mother Sasha when allowed. Four years ago, Sasha had needed Karen's calm reassurance desperately, and she never forgot how much she owed her sister-in-law. Karen had pulled her through a black depression simply by remaining her warm, loving, untroubled self—Sasha had been drowning and Karen had carried her to safety, almost without knowing what she was doing.

Karen was still watching her, and as if she had read her thoughts in her eyes, she said suddenly: 'You're over it, aren't you? I thought you'd never get over him, but you have. Do you ever think of him now?' From anyone else the question would have been an intolerable intrusion, but Karen was licensed by the past. Sasha gave her a wry smile.

'Now and then, when the moon is blue . . .' It was half a joke, but said with bittersweet acceptance of all she was not saying.

The kettle boiled and Karen turned hurriedly to make the tea; she was uneasy with such discussions, although she was always ready to listen if Sasha needed a sympathetic ear.

Billy came in from the shop, rubbing his hands and chuckling. 'He bought them; didn't even haggle—for his old mum, he said, back in Elkhorn, Nebraska; they'll look fantastic on her dining-room table when she has her friends to lunch.' He peered at the cup Karen was handing him. 'Ah, tea, just what I need. Now that was a nice guy, he didn't looked bored when I told him how to keep them looking as good as they do now, he even thanked me for my little leaflet. I hope his mum likes her present—she should. I was half sorry to see those two go.'

'If you had your way we'd never sell anything,' Karen scolded indulgently, and he ruffled her brown hair, grinning.

'Have you two decided whether Sasha's starting work here again?'

'She's had another offer,' Karen told him. 'And I think she should take that—in a roundabout sort of way it could help her career.'

Sasha laughed. 'How do you make that out?'

'This Mrs Fox is a friend of Jake Redway's, isn't she?'

'If gossip is to be believed, she's rather more than that,' Sasha said unguardedly, then wished she hadn't opened her big mouth as Karen stared at her.

'You didn't say they were having an affair!'

'I don't know that they are,' Sasha said wryly. 'They're very close, that much I could see for myself, and Maggie did let slip something . . . but I might have misinterpreted, it could all be smoke and no fire.'

'Jake Redway,' Billy mused, nursing his tea with both hands. 'Isn't he the fellow with eyebrows?'

Sasha chuckled. 'We all have those, but yes, I know what you mean—he does have very striking eyebrows.'

'Cartoonists always go very heavily on them when they do him,' Billy said. 'They look like moustaches that have got into the wrong place.'

'Blasphemy,' said Karen, punching his arm. 'Winged and satanic, a columnist called them in *The Globe* the other day.'

'*That* was a woman,' Billy said. 'No man would lower himself to such idiocy.'

'That's the last cup of tea I make *you*,' Karen told him. 'Rank chauvinism!' He winked at her and she laughed. 'And don't try to get round me like that! I'm a Redway fan, I've seen all his films, and I think he's gorgeous. He's a real man, he has more sex appeal in his little finger than . . .'

'Me in my whole body?' Billy queried complacently, leaning against the sink, his long thin body relaxed.

'You'll do,' said Karen, her mouth curving at his wicked self-satisfaction. 'I think Sasha should see Mrs Fox, though. It won't do her any harm to be working for one of Jake Redway's buddies, whether they're having an affair or not. It might mean she'll meet a big film director and . . .'

'What a romantic you are,' said Billy, his eyes loving. 'If Redway is as sexy as you seem to think, Sasha might be well advised to stay clear of him.'

Sasha laughed angrily. 'You're got to be kidding—I'm in no danger from Jake Redway, believe me. He's not on my list of men I'd like to make it with . . .'

'Really, Sasha!' Karen protested, laughing.

'Billy, put your hands over your ears, you're too young to hear this.'

He obeyed, amused. 'I'm going back to my silver-polishing,' he said. 'If I stay around here much longer my innocent mind might be corrupted . . .' He wanted out, and Sasha glanced up at the ceiling as there was a crash and an outraged wail.

'That sounds like Robby—I'll go up and see them, I feel like a game of Space Invaders to take my mind off my troubles.'

As she walked to the door which led out at the foot of the stairs, Karen asked: 'Will you see Mrs Fox?' and Sasha looked back, nodding.

'I might as well,' she said, and as she said it knew that she had intended to do so before she came here. She had already decided what she would do last night, but talking to Karen and Billy had, as it always did, helped to clarify her mind.

When she rang Mrs Fox later a man answered, his voice coolly contained. 'Who is it speaking?' he asked when Sasha asked for Mrs Fox, and there was something in his tone which made her stammer as though she was guilty of something.

'My name is Sasha Lewis, Mr Redway suggested that I . . .'

'Redway?' The question cut into her husky words like a steel blade, icily destructive, and she flushed.

'I'm looking for a job and . . . I gathered your wife needed help with the baby?' She was certain it was James Fox, remembering what Maggie had said about him.

There was a pause, then he said curtly: 'Hold on, please.'

A moment later Caroline Fox said with far more

warmth: 'Miss Lewis? Oh, it is good of you to ring. I was hoping you'd take me up on my idea, I do hope you're going to say yes.'

Sasha felt herself relaxing. 'Well, I'd certainly like to talk about it . . .'

'Marvellous! Could you come down here to see Madeleine and my house? You ought to get a look at what you'd be taking on!' Caro Fox had easy laughter in her voice, clearly she felt sure that nobody could resist her little girl once they saw her, and Sasha's mouth curved in an answering smile.

'I'd like that. When . . .'

'Why not tomorrow, if that's convenient?'

'Fine,' said Sasha. She wrote down the name of the village and the nearest railway station, Caroline Fox suggested several train times which would get her there in time for lunch and took her private telephone number and address. Sasha put down the phone and danced into the shop where Billy and Karen were working.

'I'm going there tomorrow,' she said. 'I've got a feeling I'm going to find her husband pretty heavy going, but she's a darling.'

'Where do they live?' asked Billy, and made a face when Sasha told him. 'How are you going to get back to London every night? That's forty miles away!'

Sasha stopped dancing, her face falling. 'So it is—I hadn't thought of that.'

'Maybe they want someone to live in?' suggested Karen. 'It could be quite fun for you, Sasha, living in the country for a few weeks.'

'If you ever see any country! If this Mrs Fox doesn't keep you busy all day running about after her and her baby.' Billy sounded drily pessimistic, and his wife grimaced at him.

'Take no notice of him, he's got a sinking feeling that one of the new pieces he got at the auction isn't genuine, and at the moment every apple has got a maggot.'

'Oh, well, if he's in that sort of mood I'm off,' said Sasha, grabbing her shopping bag and making for the door. Billy yelled after her: 'Let us know what you decide to do!' and she waved back at him. 'Of course I will . . .'

She had a two-roomed furnished flat in a grimy terraced house on the wrong side of Islington, with a congested view of roofs and back walls and television aerials. Her private territory consisted of a square sitting-room which had a kitchenette at one end of it and a tiny bedroom, with a bathroom built into one corner, under the slope of the ceiling. When Sasha took a bath she had to slide into it sideways or she crashed her head on the plaster, and to get into the cupboard-like room at all she had to insert herself sideways because the door would not open wide enough to let her walk through normally. When it rained she heard water dripping up in the roof rafters, sometimes it seeped through, leaving strange damp shapes on her wall, and a sweet-rotten smell which lingered for hours. On the ground floor lived a widow of sixty-eight who had two cats which often climbed up to sit on Sasha's windowsill and stared menacingly at her, their slitted green eyes radiating curiosity and emotional blackmail. On summer evenings when the window was open they delicately stepped inside and raided her larder, the door of which would never shut properly. When they ate the

sardines she had left on a plate, meaning to have
them for supper later, she took to blocking the
door with a hefty volume of Shakespeare. Mrs
Hughes worshipped her cats, according to her they
lived on the fat of the land: chicken livers and
boiled herrings, but they always assumed a
famished, pleading look when they saw Sasha.

Above Sasha lived an Indian medical student of
impeccable good manners and sad eyes who
always looked exhausted and frequently worked
all night. He was fanatically determined to pass his
exams, his family had made great sacrifices to give
him a chance to become a doctor. When he passed
Sasha he looked down politely, but if she said
'Good morning,' he always whispered 'Good
morning' back before he vanished up into his attic.
He was so quiet she barely knew he was on the
floor above: he did not play a radio loudly or have
wild parties, his floorboards rarely creaked and he
did not bang his doors. She hoped he wouldn't
move before she did.

When she got back to her flat that Sunday
afternoon the summer air was heavy with heat.
She opened all the windows and her curtains hung
unmoving, there was no breeze, but she could
smell the scent of new-mown grass from the next
garden and when she leant on the sill to glance
down she saw Mrs Hughes working away, weeding
the cottage garden which kept her busy all year.
The two cats prowled around, tails waving over
their backs.

Sasha went into the kitchen to make herself a
long, cool drink. As she moved about she thought
of Jake Redway, her brow creasing. Why hadn't
she told Karen and Billy who he was? She had

meant to before she got to the shop that morning, she had imagined their expressions. They would have been amazed, taken aback, shaken—as she had been. She had fully intended to tell them, yet she hadn't, and she wasn't quite sure why, except that she knew how hard she found it to talk about the circumstances which had surrounded their first meeting. The events were like a bruise which, even after it has outwardly healed, leaves a tenderness on the skin. The merest brush of a fingertip could make her wince.

Sipping her drink, she changed into a bikini. She would go down to the pocket-handkerchief garden to sunbathe. Mrs Hughes was always glad to have someone to talk to, and she had stopped gardening now and was sitting in a deckchair on the square patch of lawn, knitting, a yellowing straw hat on her head.

Sasha collected a towel and a paperback book, her sunglasses and suntan oil, and opened the door of her flat just as Jake Redway appeared at the top of the stairs. Sasha was so staggered to see him that for a second or two she just froze there, staring at him, then to her own fury she found herself flushing to the hairline and clutching her possessions to her half-naked body as though to hide herself from him.

'Going somewhere?' His dry question didn't ease her tension; intensifying it as his eyes drifted down over her slender body in the brief white bikini. It was absurd to feel so selfconscious: if she had been lying on a sunny beach among a crowd of other sunbathers she would have been totally unaware of how little she was wearing, but standing on the landing in the silent house with

Jake Redway staring at her made her want to bolt back into her flat and slam the door.

'What are you doing here?' she asked uneasily. He was casually dressed, himself, but far more concealingly—in dark blue jeans which had been pressed neatly, a very thin linen shirt which fitted his body so closely she could see the tanned body under it, a darker shadow running upward from his waist which betrayed black body hair. The shirt was open at the throat, the lapels laid back and between them smooth brown skin.

'Maggie gave me your address.' He took a step forward and she automatically backed into the flat.

'What did you want to see me about?'

He closed the front door and glanced around the sitting-room. 'Do you live here alone?'

She reacted to the question angrily, eyes flashing. 'Yes, I do!'

The vehemence made him look back at her, brows lifting. 'No need to get into a temper, it was a straightforward question. You're too touchy, Miss Lewis, you read too much into polite small talk.' He wasn't so much commenting on the present as on her behaviour at the last night party, she realised; the blue eyes were coldly ironic and derisive, she did not like their expression—but then she did not like anything much about Jake Redway.

She felt stupid standing there clutching her little pile of belongings, so she put them down on the table, aware all the time of his scrutiny. He was a man who always made women aware of their sexuality, she thought, remembering how a brief glance from those blue eyes had made her feel when he appeared at the door of the dressing-room and saw her in her bra and panties.

When she turned back to him he was staring even more intently, his black brows drawn together in a frown. 'Where have I seen you before?' he asked as if talking to himself. 'Where on earth was it?'

Sasha's heart constricted, she took a sharp breath. 'You said you wanted to see me about something,' she stammered hurriedly, hoping to sidetrack him.

'In that bikini,' he muttered. 'A bikini . . .'

'You're not making any sense to me, Mr Redway. Do you have a message for me from Mrs Fox?' She prayed that her uneasiness would not show in her manner.

He ran a hand through his dark brown hair, shrugging. 'It will come to me sooner or later. Yes, Caro tells me you're coming down to see her tomorrow. I offered to drive you down.'

'There's no need, I can get the train,' Sasha said quickly.

'Why bother when I can drive you?'

'I like train journeys.' She was struggling to control a rising sense of alarm, it was ridiculous to feel so threatened simply because he was offering to drive her there, but she couldn't disguise the tremor in her voice. She could not bear to sit in a car with Jake Redway for several hours, she couldn't face the prospect.

'Don't be absurd,' he retorted. She coloured, trembling.

'Please, Mr Redway, there's no . . .'

'My God!' he muttered, his voice altering dramatically. She looked into the bright blue eyes and saw them widening, the black pupils hard and clear. Sasha felt dizzy as it dawned on her what that stare meant.

'I know who you are,' he said slowly, and she swallowed, an agitated pulse beating in the hollow at the base of her throat. 'God knows how I failed to recognise you before.' He slowly studied her from her pale face down the whole length of the slender body, but without the disturbing element of sexual appraisal which had made her flush earlier. His expression now was thoughtful, surprised, taken aback, but it was none of those reactions which troubled Sasha—it was another emotion altogether which was showing in his face, a feeling she rejected violently and which appalled her. Jake Redway's hard face had softened with compassion, and Sasha feared pity, it weakened her, she shunned it in self-defence, and from a defensive frown swung into aggression, her hands curling into fists at her side.

'It was very kind of you to offer to drive me to Mrs Fox's house, but I'd rather make my own way there, Mr Redway.' She opened the front door again and stood back, waiting.

He moved, but not to leave. He pushed the door shut despite the fact that she was hanging on to the door handle like grim death.

'You knew me right away, I suppose,' he said coolly.

Sasha gave up. Head bent, she muttered: 'Quite soon, yes.'

'You never gave a hint of recognition.' He was talking casually, yet she could feel him watching her and she sensed that he was working out her motives in his mind.

'There seemed no point in saying anything.' It was an evasive answer to a sentence which hadn't been a question, merely a comment. 'I prefer to bury the past,' she added with a surge of something like desperation, hoping he would stop probing and go away.

'I went to the hospital to see you the next day, but they told me you couldn't have visitors,' he said. 'I had to fly to the States that evening; I sent you some flowers—did you get them?'

She had handed them back to the nurse, who had looked shocked and disapproving until Sasha told her to give them to someone who had no flowers, then the girl had remembered that Sasha was distraught and had gone away, smiling soothingly. She had not seen Sasha tear up the card which had come with the flowers; Sasha had not even read it, she had not wanted to know the name of the man who had both saved her life and wrecked it in one act.

'I was very sorry about your husband,' Jake Redway said, watching her. 'I felt like hell about it for weeks, but I didn't have time to weigh up the situation properly, you know. I saw you in the water, I had to act fast—I had no idea you weren't alone.'

Sasha couldn't trust her voice; she stared downwards, stubbornly silent. Why was he insisting on talking about it when he must realise she did not want to remember? Whenever she tried to think about that day her mind broke up into piercing, glittering fragments of pain and incredulity; she saw the blue-green seas crashing down in a curling wave topped white with flying spray and flung from them a bare brown arm, the hand splayed. It was the last she had ever seen of Philip, and each time she remembered it she felt such anguish that she jerked away and made herself think about other things.

'Don't cry,' Jake Redway said suddenly, abrupt dismay in his voice, and it was only then that she felt the wetness on her lashes; she had not even realised that tears had come into her eyes. 'I didn't mean to upset you.' Before she could brush a hand over her face he had put an arm around her, pulling her towards him. Sasha struggled angrily, but he held her, pressing her face into his shoulder with one hand while the other gently stroked her spine, as if she was an unhappy child he was comforting. There was nothing remotely sexual about the movement, but Sasha trembled.

She hated being in his arms, it reminded her too vividly of the last time he had held her; she had fought him, struggling and screaming like a crazy woman as he tried to drag her into his boat. 'No! Not me! Get Philip first!' The wind had carried her words away and she had not heard what Jake Redway was saying, either; she had only seen his wet brown features looming over her, his face harsh with determination, his lips moving as he shouted down to her but the words lost in the tumult of wind and waves.

Then he had hit her, his punch leaving a dark bruise on her jaw for days afterwards. She had slumped, and when she recovered consciousness she was lying face down on the deck of his boat, coughing and shuddering. He was kneeling over her, she felt his firm hands gripping her bare midriff. When she began to struggle up he held her down.

'No, lie still for a while, you're exhausted. I'll get a jacket for you,' he had said.

Sasha had struggled to her knees, throwing off his grip, sobbing: 'My husband, Philip, he's in the water!' She had seen Jake Redway's face alter, the brown skin glistening with spray, the blue eyes stunned and dark, then he had leapt to the side of the boat and she had stumbled after him, her eyes searching the empty horizon in despair.

'Swing round, he must be there!'

They had circled again and again, but there had been no sign of Philip; he had gone, only the drifting, upturned boat in which they had set out for a summer afternoon's sail had shown her where she had last seen him. When Jake Redway gently told her there was no point in searching any longer, they must stail back to port themselves before it was dark, she had turned on him like a wildcat. She had been clinging to the boat, she could have stayed afloat for ages, there had been no hurry about saving her. Philip had been flung outwards as the boat heeled over; he had never been a very strong swimmer, he hadn't been able to make it back to her, each time he tried a wave had smashed him back. Jake had listened, frowning.

'I told you to get him first; if you'd listened to me he needn't have . . .' She had choked into weeping silence and heard Jake sigh.

'I didn't hear what you were saying, I thought you were crazy with shock. I'm sorry.' He had tried to put his arms around her then and she had flung him back, screaming to him not to touch her, to stay away from her. Jake had sailed back to land in silence while she sat, wrapped in a blanket and jacket, shivering and ice-cold, slowly becoming more and more withdrawn as time went by.

She had had a very happy childhood, she had grown up secure and confident and she had met, fallen in love with and married Philip by the time she was twenty. She had felt so adult, so certain of herself, her whole life had seemed sunlit—nothing had prepared her for the trauma of Philip's death. In many ways, perhaps, she had still been a child; expecting happiness as if it was her birthright, life had seemed like a happy dream to her. She had been cruelly enlightened.

She broke out of the painful memories she had not wanted to live through again, and pushed Jake Redway from her, her face set and white. He stared down at her, his brows drawn. 'You don't still blame me for your husband's death, for God's sake?' he asked curtly, reading the bitterness in her straight mouth. Sasha didn't answer, she knew with one part of her mind that he was not to blame for anything, it had been a tragic accident and she owed him her life, but she couldn't bear the sight of him all the same. She never would be able to, every time she saw him she would be reminded of what had happened, feel the same intolerable pang of grief, despair and incredulity.

Turning shakily, she opened the door again. 'Please, I can't talk any more—would you go?'

For a second or two she thought he was going to argue, she felt tension in him and averted her head, shuddering; she could not bear any more, she would break down and cry if he didn't go and she hated the thought of losing control of herself while he was there, watching her, as he had watched her on that boat as she screamed and wept. There had been something naked about those moments; she had felt sick afterwards, remembering them, remembering him watching her with pity. She rejected his pity, she did not want him to know how badly she had been hurt, she did not want anyone to know.

But he didn't say any more, he walked past her without a word, and Sasha shut the door and leaned on it, shuddering from head to foot.

CHAPTER THREE

AFTER studying Mrs Fox's suggested train times, Sasha decided to catch the later train because it was a fast train; the others all stopped at every station and took hours. Next morning was very misty, the sky veiled in pearl in which a hazy sun glowed like a ragged marigold. Sasha wanted to make a good impression, not so much on Mrs Fox who had already seen her in her bra and panties without a flicker of surprise, but on this icy-voiced husband who was so unpopular with Maggie, so she very carefully chose what she would wear. A pleated linen dress, white, with navy-blue and crimson stripes finely running from shoulder to hem and crimson buttons, seemed suitably formal and demure. She brushed her thick black curls back and glossed her lips with a lipstick which matched the red stripes, looking at herself in her mirror with amused satisfaction. It was acting, of a sort; creating an image of herself which James Fox would approve. Clothes were vital to that, most people typed you by your clothes, especially in busy cities where nobody has time to think too deeply about the people they meet. They assess the outer shell you show them and often miss what is inside it.

She left the house in good time to catch her train, but stopped dead on the pavement as the gate clanged shut behind her. A car was parked opposite with Jake Redway behind the wheel. He leaned over to open the passenger door, it swung back and Sasha slowly walked over, frowning.

She did not get in, she bent and looked at him, her blue eyes flickering uneasily. 'Mr Redway, I told you . . .'

'Get in and don't be so damned silly.' The tone was impatient, she saw his long fingers tapping a restless rhythm on the wheel.

For a few seconds she thought about it, considering what to do: she could walk off down the street to the tube station, but he might follow her, kerb-crawling beside her, and that would be embarrassing. She could argue her right to make her own travel arrangements, but he would obviously override her views. She had made herself very clear last night, but here he was this morning. Jake Redway, as she had bitter reason to remember, was a man who took no notice of what you said to him, however vehemently you said it, he just went ahead and did things his way, regardless.

Sasha got into the car and closed the door. He glanced sideways, triumph in every line of him, and she turned to stare back, the nape of her neck prickling with irritation.

'Mr Redway . . .'

'Jake,' he interrupted.

She ignored him. 'Mr Redway, one day it's going to dawn on you that you aren't God, and I hope the shock won't be too much for you.'

'How kind,' he said, starting the car, his hard mouth amused. 'I'm touched by your concern for me.'

'Go to hell,' Sasha muttered, turning her head to stare out of the side window.

'Make up your mind,' he drawled. 'First I'm God, now I'm the devil . . . are you some kind of religious fruitcake, Miss Lewis?'

She decided to ignore that, too. Instead, she asked: 'How did you know what time I'd be leaving? Or have you been parked out there for hours?'

He stared straight ahead at the traffic thronging the busy main road leading south towards the river. 'It was easy—I looked at the timetable and decided anyone with any sense would take the fast train. I guessed it would take you half an hour to get to Waterloo by tube from your flat, so I worked out that if I arrived here an hour before the train left I'd be sure to pick you up on the wing.'

Sasha laughed angrily. 'Clever!' She looked round to go on and saw his profile with a sudden sense of shock. He was a man who surprised your eyes, at times his face harsh and rawboned, far from handsome, but then abruptly altering to radiate a powerful sexuality. Seen like that, in strong sunlight, his tanned skin smoothly shaven, his eyes half hidden by lowered lids, their colour merely a vivid slit of bright blue, his mouth lazily cynical and his jawline firm and determined, he was eye-riveting. She felt winded as it occurred to her that she was sitting in a car with Jake Redway. Millions of women across the world would envy her and be more than ready to swap places with her. She had been so obsessed with the dark memory he represented for her that it had only just dawned on her that he was a very famous man, brilliantly successful in his career, certainly very rich and much pursued by her own sex.

Until that moment her image of him had been distinctly one-dimensional—he was the man who had been part of the most agonising experience she had ever had, she had blindly hated him, and it had not been personal, she hadn't even known his name. Frowning, she concentrated on her own emotions. No, it had not been hatred, that was only the nearest word which could describe the blackness of her feelings about him. She had almost wished he had not intervened, that he had let her drown with her husband. She had not felt grateful because she did not want to live without Philip, she had confusedly rejected the life which Jake Redway had given back to her, and him with it. In her pain and despairing rage she had thought of him as though he was an inanimate object which she had kicked against, like a child furiously kicking the chair against which it has stubbed its toe.

When she first met him again that was still how she felt. She had looked at him with an echo of the old bitterness, she hadn't yet fixed his identity in her mind as a separate part of him, he had not been Jake Redway, famous film star, he had been *that* man, the faceless unknown who had snatched her from the cruel sea and in doing so had broken the bond between herself and Philip.

This morning she felt that image dissolving into his own real personality. He was not an inanimate object, he was a human being with charisma and status, a sexually powerful male animal with charm and humour cloaking the stark self-will which she had seen in operation long ago.

'Are you sulking?'

The mocking question broke into her thoughts,

and she looked up and saw that they were moving slowly across London Bridge in a nose-to-tail line of vehicles. Below them the Thames glittering in sunshine, as blue as Jake Redway's eyes.

'I was thinking,' she defended, glancing into those eyes and seeing a teasing smile in them.

'Not before time,' he said drily.

'Why did you want to drive me down to Millton?' As she asked the question she watched him closely and saw the flicker of quick assessment he gave her, then his lids dropped down, he turned to look ahead again, his features coolly remote.

'I had a free day and thought it would be fun to drive into the country.'

Sasha thought about the gossip she had heard. 'Is Mr Fox going to be there?'

A faint stain of dark red crept up his face. 'I've no idea.'

Sasha didn't believe him—if there *was* fire behind all the smoke, Jake Redway would jump at any excuse to see Caroline Fox without her husband guessing what was going on between them, but from James Fox's icy response when she mentioned Jake's name his suspicions were already aroused and Jake would need a really convincing excuse.

'I don't like being used,' she said, and heard him take a harsh breath.

'*What* did you say?' The question snapped at her, startling her, it was bitten out too clearly for her to ignore.

'Don't use me as a cover for whatever you're up to,' she muttered.

'Who the hell d'you think you are?' he flared back, his hands gripping the wheel so tightly she saw their strong bones in pronounced outline under the brown skin. 'Don't stand in judgement on me, Miss Lewis, because you don't have the right, it's none of your business why I want to drive over to see Caro—and you can take that look off your face, you're jumping to damned unpleasant conclusions without any idea what you're dealing with. You may see everything in black and white, but the world's coloured in half-tones you're too blind to see.'

Sasha laughed with answering anger. There had been a contemptuous sting in his voice which had irritated her. 'Are you calling me unsophisticated?' She gave the word a scornful emphasis.

'I'm telling you to mind your own damned business,' he retorted.

'That's fine by me, I'm not interested in your affairs,' and Sasha used the last word with icy deliberation. 'Just don't involve me in future.'

He didn't answer this time, but his silence was loaded with rage she could feel, he was breathing heavily, each rough intake of air audible in the car. Sasha studied the grey huddle of London suburbs they were passing through and surreptitiously glanced at her watch. How much longer would it take to get to Millton?

It was forty minutes before the car pulled off a narrow Kent road, running between high green hedges alive with birds, into a gravelled drive leading to an elegant white Georgian house. The wheels crunched to a halt in front of the portico, the front door opened and Caroline Fox appeared, smiling; red-gold hair feathered across her pale temples, green eyes giving vivacity to a face which was far too delicate.

Jake got out and Sasha slowly followed in time to see Caroline run to meet him and hug him, kissing his cheek with both arms round his neck. That wasn't all she saw—it all happened very fast, she noticed things which only later did she remember and add up—like Jake's hands coming up to grasp Caro's waist, his eyes half-closing as she kissed him, a tense line around his mouth, pulling his face into a mask of wry awareness. The next minute Caroline Fox swung round and smiled at Sasha.

'It's good of you to come, did you have a nice drive? You must need a drink by now—Jake is the world's scariest driver, he takes hair-raising risks!'

'Slander,' Jake said, grinning.

'Darling, you know you enjoy taking risks! It raises your blood sugar or something.'

Jake looked at Sasha over his shoulder as he walked into the house. 'I think she means adrenalin—with Caro you can never be quite sure what she's talking about.'

Caroline linked arms with Sasha, smiling at her. 'Did he drive like a fiend all the way down here? Come on, don't be nervous—Jake may be the big star everywhere else, but here he's just my old buddy Donald Duck.'

Sasha's brows shot up. 'Donald Duck?'

Caro laughed. 'Haven't you heard him do his Donald Duck voice? He's famous for it—go on, Jake, show Sasha how good you are.'

He looked round impatiently, shaking his head. 'Don't be an idiot! How about that drink you were talking about?'

'Keep your hair on—I'll get it for you,' said Caroline as she and Sasha followed him into the spacious, quietly furnished hall which had oak panelling on the walls and polished red tiling on the floors, jewel-coloured rugs scattered here and there across the surface. Sasha looked down at them and Caro followed her gaze, smiling.

'Turkish,' she said. 'We got them in Istanbul last year, aren't they lovely?' Jake had vanished into another room, they heard him opening a cabinet and then the clink of glasses.

'Make yourself at home, won't you?' invited Caro, walking away from Sasha, who thought for a moment she was addressing her, only to realise a second later that Caro was talking to Jake, her voice sarcastic.

Sasha slowly walked after Caro and paused on the threshold of a rectangular sitting-room, furnished in springlike green and white; the carpet deep white pile on which footsteps showed briefly before the impression faded, the curtains an apple green and the deep-upholstered modern chintz chairs and couch a mixture of the two. It was an elegant room, but a very comfortable family one, meant to be lived in rather than just looked at; on every surface stood silver-framed photos of family and friends or stylishly chosen porcelain pieces which perfectly matched the décor, or white china table lamps with pretty green or pink shades.

'What can I get you, Sasha?' Caro asked. 'Gin and tonic, sherry, a Martini?'

'A dry sherry, please,' Sasha answered, looking around her.

As Caro put the glass into her hand she said mischievously: 'Madeleine is eating her lunch in the kitchen . . .'

'Not a pretty sight,' said Jake, grinning, and Caro laughed.

'She's improving—she gets most of it into her mouth now instead of painting her face with it!' She waved a hand to one of the chairs. 'Do sit down, Sasha, you look as if you're poised to flee, standing there like that.'

Sasha sat down, her glass of sherry held carefully. Jake was prowling around the room as restlessly as a caged animal, picking up photos and staring at them. He passed in front of her chair, staring at her briefly, and she saw hostility in his blue eyes. He was still angry after the row they had had on the way down here. Well, great—she hoped he had taken note of what she said. She had meant it, he was not using her as cover for a secret relationship with a married woman. It was none of her business what he and Caro Fox did, but it certainly was her business if they tried to involve her in their problems.

'Shall we discuss the job before lunch, during lunch or afterwards?' Caro asked her, smiling as she sat down on a chair beside her.

'We might as well . . .'

'Get it out of the way now? I agree. Well, basically what I need is someone who will help with Madeleine during the day. The problem is the travelling—I hadn't worked out the details, that hadn't occurred to me, but my husband, James, pointed out that you had to get to and from London each day. The first train leaves Waterloo at some unearthly hour, there are plenty of others after that—it could be done, but it would cost a lot in terms of time and money, not to mention the wear and tear on the nerves. If you'd prefer that,

that's fine with me, but if you like the idea we do have a spare room, a very nice one, and we'd be happy to have you use that while you're working for us. You could have weekends off, I'd cope with Madeleine at weekends. And, of course, any evening during the week . . .' Caro paused, slightly breathless; she had rushed into the long proposition with a nervous, coaxing manner, as though afraid Sasha would turn it down.

'I'd be happy to fall in with either plan,' Sasha said. 'Obviously the travelling would be tiring, but I expect I could manage—but if you really don't mind if I stay here during the week. . . .'

'It would suit me very well,' Caro said frankly, relaxing. 'James works so hard, I barely see him from one week's end to the next, it would be fun to have you here.'

Jake had stopped wandering about and was standing by the open french windows, occasionally drinking his whisky, listening to them.

'Are you experienced with babies?' Caro asked.

Sasha hesitated. 'I have two nephews, I've babysat with them many times.'

'Would it make your nervous if I went out and left you alone with Madeleine occasionally? Please, be frank—I'd like to be able to go up to town and have lunch with my husband or Maggie or a friend from time to time.'

'Once Madeleine is used to me I'm sure I'd be more than happy to fall in with any plans you had,' Sasha said slightly stiffly, thinking: for friend do I read Jake Redway? Did Caroline Fox want to have the day free now and then so that she could go up to town and have secret meetings with him? She looked into the other woman's eyes and saw no shadow of double meaning in them, they were as clear and bright as a child's, their gaze directly frank. Sasha looked towards Jake and he was staring down into his glass, his black brows knitted.

Caroline began to talk about her child then and Sasha listened hard, watching her and reminding herself that this woman, like herself, was an actress, trained in the art of lying with utter conviction. Even the open frankness of her eyes could not be trusted. Caroline would not be much of an actress if she could not dissemble too well to be doubted, she knew how to project the right impression.

'We ought to discuss money,' Caroline said wryly. She suggested a sum which surprised Sasha, it was far more generous than she had expected.

'That would be fine,' Sasha said quickly. It meant she would be able to pay her rent while she was here and keep her flat to go back to at weekends. She would be eating here, would have no fares to pay, all her living expenses would be cut to the bone during her stay. She might even be able to save some money from what was left after she had paid her rent.

Caroline relaxed back in her chair, sighing. 'Well, that's wonderful. Was there anything you wanted to ask me?'

Sasha shook her head. 'I can't think of anything.' Or, at least, anything she felt she could ask the other woman—Caroline's relationship with Jake Redway was no business of hers, as he had rightly pointed out. No doubt in time she would find out the truth, anyway—a love affair, however secret, always leaves visible signs. Lovers can't help looking at each other, exchanging secret signals which can be picked up by outsiders.

'Then come and meet Madeleine,' said Caroline, getting up.

Jake took Sasha's glass; she had barely touched her sherry, as his dry glance at the contents pointed out to her.

She walked after Caroline, her face blank. Lunch was going to be a difficult occasion. She already felt distinctly uneasy in their company, every glance they gave each other made her nerves prickle, not least because already she liked Caroline Fox and felt rather sorry for her, trapped between two men. Whatever Caroline felt for her husband it could not be a happy situation: each day must be charged with danger and tension—perhaps that was why Caroline had that fragile, lost air at times.

The kitchen was a square, carefully planned room full of modern furniture and gadgets with large windows on two sides allowing sunshine to flood in, illuminating the grey-haired woman at the sink and the child in a high-chair, banging a spoon on an upturned plastic mug.

Sasha looked at her and the little girl beamed, revealing small white teeth and pink gums. Her face was so happy that Sasha fell in love. Madeleine Fox, even at the age of two, had personality coming out of every pore—small and fine-boned, with her mother's heart-shaped face and big hazel eyes which looked green in the sunlight, her curly black hair dishevelled and showing fragments of rice pudding. More rice pudding decorated the lace-trimmed white bib she wore. Madeleine was enjoying herself, her round

pink fist clutched her spoon more tightly as her
mother advanced on her, and she crashed it down,
sending her mug spinning off the tray of her high-
chair.

'Say hello to Sasha, Madeleine,' said Caroline,
lifting her out of her chair after she had unclasped
the straps holding her in it.

Sasha smiled at the little girl and Madeleine
solemnly offered her the spoon. 'Thank you,' said
Sasha, taking it, feeling as though she had been
given a valuable gift.

Caroline hoisted her daughter up, Madeleine's
pink bare knees anchoring her to her mother's
waist, her arms around Caroline's neck in a
strangling grip. 'She's shy,' Caroline said.

'At two they always are,' said Sasha.

The woman at the sink had turned to observe
them, and Caroline smiled in her direction. 'This is
Sasha Lewis, Mrs Carter—she's going to help me
with Madeleine for a while.'

Mrs Carter's face was wrinkled, grey, wryly
resigned, as though life had disappointed her too
often for her to care any more, and her black eyes
watched Sasha the way the eyes of monkeys did at
the zoo, remotely, yet with sharp humour. 'A very
good idea—she's a proper handful, that one. More
energy than's good for her!'

Caroline laughed. 'More than is good for me,
anyway,' she half-agreed, then said to Sasha: 'She
has a nap after lunch—it gives us an hour's peace
and quiet, not that she always sleeps, but she does
stay quite quiet in her cot except that she chucks
her toys about all over the floor.' She took off the
bib and rapidly washed Madeleine's face.

'I'll serve the lunch now, shall I?' asked Mrs

Carter, looking at the large electric clock on the kitchen wall. Caroline was running a brush over the child's hair.

'Yes, please, Mrs Carter.' Caroline moved to the door, still carrying the child. 'I'll put Madeleine down in her cot while you're doing that.'

Sasha followed her and Caroline said over her shoulder: 'We're having melon and ham salad—I hope that's okay with you.'

'It sounds delicious, very cooling. Hasn't the weather been incredible? I wonder how much longer we can expect these temperatures?'

They were making polite small talk because they did not know each other well enough to do anything else. Sasha went up the stairs with mother and child, noticing the pretty wallpaper on the walls beside her, a very pale pink stripe on silky white paper which was very slightly shot with silver, the metallic hint only visible when the sun shone from one angle.

Madeleine's room was quiet and already shady, the cotton blinds drawn down to exclude the bright sun. Caroline took off her daughter's little white shoes and laid her down in her pink cot, handing her a large floppy rag doll, which Madeleine clutched close to her. Caroline bent over to kiss her, then the two women softly tiptoed out.

'Just come and take a peek at the room you'll have,' invited Caroline, turning down the corridor. She opened a door at the end of it and walked forward, Sasha at her heels. It was a charming bedroom furnished in shades of white and lilac, far more spacious than the bedroom in Sasha's flat and a great deal more elegant. 'Is it okay?'

Caroline asked, watching her face as Sasha glanced around.

'It's fabulous,' said Sasha, eyes wry. 'You should see the dump I live in—the rooms are so small my friends have to visit me in instalments!'

Caroline laughed. 'I can imagine— how I remember theatre digs! Grubby, shabby and smelling of cabbage and disinfectant.'

Their eyes met and Sasha felt the same warmth she had felt when Caro came to the dressing-room on their last night.

'Do you ever regret leaving the profession?'

'Constantly!'

'Then why don't you . . .'

Caroline grimaced, interrupting the impulsive question: 'I couldn't manage a career and a family. I know some women do it with one hand tied behind their back, but I'm not a superwoman, it would break me in half to try. Anyway, James . . .' She broke off, her lashes fluttering down over her green eyes. 'Lunch will be ready,' she said, turning back to the door, and leaving Sasha with a flurry of questions to which she guessed she would get no answer if she asked them.

On the stairs, Caroline asked her: 'It only just occurred to me—I hope this arrangement won't wreck your private life? I mean, if your boyfriend ever wants to pop down to see you he's very welcome.'

'Thank you,' Sasha said unrevealingly. There was no one special in her life, she had occasionally dated someone during the past two years, but none of the men she had gone out with had ever really made an impression on her. She had liked them, or she wouldn't have dated them in the first place, but Sasha had a deep sense of the integrity of loving, she preferred to be alone and possibly lonely rather than to fill the corners of her life with people she did not truly care about.

'I've laid out on the terrace,' Mrs Carter said to them from the kitchen door, wiping her wet hands on a towel.

'Thank you, Mrs Carter,' said Caroline Fox, then put her head round the door of the sitting-room, 'Jake, lunch!'

He came at once, and Sasha was oddly surprised by the sight of him—as if she had forgotten he was there or had forgotten what he looked like in the interim period.

'You look very elegant,' Caroline commented, eyeing him in his lightweight grey suit and silk shirt in a paler shade of the same colour. 'Going on somewhere afterwards?'

He dwarfed her, a good head taller, his lean, muscled body moving with a calculated grace of which Sasha was impatiently aware. He moved as though always conscious of being watched, she thought.

'I'm dressed for a day in the country,' he said mockingly, grinning down at Caroline, his blue eyes intimate. 'You look very sexy yourself.'

'I look like hell,' Caroline said frankly. 'My hair's a mess and this dress has been to the cleaner's once too often.' Sasha stared at the dress, it looked very good on that slender figure, whatever Caroline might say, and the colour of it muted the vibrancy of her red-gold head.

They walked ahead, talking, and Sasha trudged in their wake, feeling excluded again, as she had in the dressing-room. They interrupted each other, laughed, used gnomic half sentences which each perfectly understood, their comprehension deeper than the words they exchanged or the constant glances and smiles which said so much more.

That intimacy irritated, like a thorn under the skin; Sasha wondered how Caroline's husband liked to watch their casual understanding. She barely knew either of them, or cared whether they talked to her or not, yet all the same she felt an angry prickle of jealousy or something very like it; their intense absorption in each other made her self-esteem wince. It is never pleasant to be part of a threesome when two of the three are so wrapped up in each other that they never notice you.

They had emerged on a paved terrace behind the house, green lawns rolling away from the stone balustrade running in a semi-circle around the terrace. Under a fluttering, striped red and green umbrella stood a table laid for lunch, with a wooden bowl of salad, a covered dish, glasses and cutlery, and at each place a boat-shaped wedge of yellowy-green melon decorated with a piece of orange threaded through with a wooden cocktail stick topped by a cherry.

Caroline glanced round. 'Sasha, why don't you sit here between us? Then we can both talk to you.'

Jake pulled back one of the white-painted iron chairs whose spoon-shaped backs were decorated with elaborate curlicues of ironwork. Caroline avoided his glance and sat down on the soft, padded cushion striped the same colours as the umbrella. They each took a chair on either side of her. Jake leaned over and lifted a bottle of white wine from the ice-filled silver bucket, deftly wrapped a white napkin around it and poured a little into his glass. He tasted it, said: 'Nice—what is it?' and glanced at the label.

'Chablis,' Caroline told him. 'Is that okay for you, Sasha?'

'I'm no wine buff,' said Sasha, feeling mutinous in the face of their duo. Jake gave her a hard stare, perhaps catching the note of resentment in her voice, then poured wine into her glass, his shoulder touching her own for a moment. She pointedly moved and was given another hard look untinged by humour.

'Tell us all about your film,' Caroline invited as he filled her glass, moving round behind Sasha to do so.

'No shop talk,' Jake said flatly, returning to his own seat.

Sasha began to eat her melon, it was icy and delicately flavoured. Across her the other two talked about Maggie. 'It's time she had a baby,' Caroline said. 'She's been married for nearly two years, how much longer is she going to wait? She can afford a year off.'

'Don't interfere,' Jake warned. 'Maggie's an adult—if she wants to wait that's her affair.'

Sasha glanced sideways at him through her lashes, her face sarcastic, and caught him glancing at her, his expression amused. He was lecturing Caroline in exactly the same way that he had talked to Sasha on the drive down here, and of course he was quite right; how other people chose to live was no concern of anyone but themselves.

Mrs Carter came out and removed their melon shells. 'Delicious,' Caroline told her, and Jake and Sasha murmured agreement. In turn they helped themselves to salad and a slice of moist, pink ham. Caroline told them that she had mixed the salad dressing herself and tossed the salad in it.

'No garlic,' she said with a teasing look at Jake. 'I wouldn't want to ruin your love life.'

'What love life?' he retorted with a flick of those dark lashes, his eyes gleaming behind them mockingly.

'Did you go to drama school straight from the sixth form, Sasha?' asked Caroline as they drank their freshly ground coffee later.

Sasha stiffened. 'No,' she admitted. 'I worked for my brother, he has an antique shop.' She did not mention her brief marriage, but she was conscious of Jake Redway watching her and she knew he was waiting for her to do so.

'Were you saving up to pay for yourself at drama school, or couldn't you get a place at first?' Caro asked.

'I was marking time,' Sasha said evasively, not adding that she had been waiting to get married. Her parents had refused to permit their marriage until she was twenty, Philip had been twenty-five when they met, and the seven years gap in age had seemed too wide to Mr and Mrs Lewis. After Philip's death Sasha had often felt bitterly resentful about that. She had felt cheated of two years of happiness, she had blamed her parents for the loss of those two years, and, although she had never openly said as much to them, she had a feeling that they had known how she felt. Some emotions cannot be concealed. Sasha had been in a mood of black despair and resentment at fate for months, even her silence had been angry.

During those first months she had been

inconsolable. She would not have believed anyone who told her she would one day smile again, feel happy, be glad to be alive. The pain had sunk into her like black ink sinking down through clear water, colouring her whole mind, and she had not turned to her parents for comfort or support, she had gone to Karen and Billy, because they had been sympathetic when Mr and Mrs Lewis refused their permission for the marriage. Billy had tried to persuade his parents to cut the two years' waiting down to one, he had come close to quarrelling with them over it. He had felt a fellow feeling for his sister because his parents had not approved of his marriage to Karen, they had wanted him to wait until he had a good job and a solid future ahead of him. Mr and Mrs Lewis were very practical, down-to-earth people. Much as they loved their children they could not sympathise with what seemed to them mere folly. They had been engaged for several years before they married, why, they said blankly, could not Billy and Sasha be as sensible?

'Your family live in London?'

Caroline's question broke into her thoughts and Sasha glanced round, eyes cloudy. 'My brother does, yes, but my parents moved down to Bournemouth when my father retired.'

'Your brother is the one with two little boys?'

'Yes, aged seven and five—they gave me my babysitting experience.' She pushed her empty coffee cup away and Caroline looked at it.

'Like some more coffee?'

'No, thank you, that was delicious, but I won't have any more.' Sasha watched Jake pour himself another cup, black and sugarless; no doubt he was careful with his diet. His looks were an important part of his career, of course.

Caroline got up. 'Come and walk round the garden, it looks at its best at this time of the year.'

Sasha got to her feet, but as they walked away Caro stopped and looked in obvious astonishment at the french windows of the room leading out on to the terrace. 'James! I wasn't expecting you back for hours! Did the case end early? Did you win?'

A man strolled out through the floor-length curtains and Sasha watched him curiously. So this was James Fox! Immaculately dressed in a pin-striped suit and blue striped formal shirt with a darker blue tie, he was tall and leanly built, a little slimmer than Jake, his hair black and his eyes in the sunshine seeming to have no particular colour, their gaze half veiled by heavy lids. Somehow Sasha had expected Caroline's husband to be older, not very attractive; a cold-faced, stooped lawyer. Her vague picture of him had been miles away from the truth—James Fox was a very good-looking man, his features hard-edged and clear-cut, austere to the point of beauty, but a beauty which had the cutting iciness of a steel blade.

'I won,' he said coolly, glancing at Jake who was lounging back in his chair and watching the other man, his smile very faintly insolent. Something in James Fox's face at that instant made Sasha certain that James Fox always won, both in court and out of it, not merely because of his personality but because he was a man to whom winning mattered. Her eyes moved on to Caroline, who was nervously winding a lock of red-gold hair around her finger, like a scolded child. What am I getting myself into? Sasha thought. This house is like a bridge over an abyss, you have to watch where you put your feet to make sure you don't fall over the edge, but what would happen if the bridge collapsed? The vibrating tensions between the other three sounded unbearably loud to her already, and at the moment she was still an outsider, looking in at them. If she moved in here she might find herself being dragged into their triangular disharmony, and she was appalled by the idea.

CHAPTER FOUR

'Why on earth didn't you tell us?' asked Karen in tones of bafflement, pressing down hard on a pleated white shirt of Billy's that she was ironing after he had worn it at a formal dinner that week. Sometimes Sasha wondered how her sister-in-law managed her life: looking after the flat upstairs above the shop, running around after the children, helping Billy with the antique silver. Karen was a one-woman industry, she burnt up time and energy while you watched in amazement, and she looked very good on it, it suited her.

'I don't know.' She was being honest, she didn't really know why she had kept it to herself that she had met the man who had pulled her from the sea.

'It's incredible—Jake Redway! You must have seen pictures of him since—surely you recognised him before now?'

'No, I never did—if I ever saw any photographs of him I didn't connect him with what happened. It took several minutes before I recognised him in the flesh.'

'Amazing,' said Karen, and deftly laid Billy's shirt on the pile of finished ironing while she watched, eyes rapt with the hypnotised fascination one always feels when someone else is working. Karen's movements had that ritualistic smoothness, she had it down to a fine art, she ironed as though it was some sort of ballet she had performed a million times before.

'I don't like the sound of this, though—nasty things, triangles. You don't want to get mixed up in anything like that. This Mr Fox sounds pretty tough.'

'He's a bit scary,' Sasha agreed. 'But I like her, and the little girl's a darling—I've accepted now, I can't back out.'

'Why do you get yourself into such muddles? Are you certain you aren't imagining things? Are they having an affair or just good friends?' Karen giggled, her eyes brilliant. 'There must be a better way of putting it than that! Pure cliché.'

'The truth often is—Karen, I don't know how much fire there is and how much is smoke. I couldn't ask them, now could I? All I know is that James Fox reacted to seeing Jake like someone spotting a slug in his salad; flared nostrils, icy eyes, the lot. And as for Jake Redway, he was acting for all he was worth . . . almost as if he was asking Mr Fox to punch him on the nose, the way he was smiling at him was pure coat-trailing. Whatever the truth, one thing's certain, those two do *not* like each other.'

Karen looked worried. 'Was he okay with you, this Mr Fox?'

'Polite,' Sasha said, remembering James Fox's long assessing stare, his firm handshake and distant courtesy. 'I wouldn't say he flipped his lid over me, I got the feeling he would have been a lot icier if he had taken against me, so I imagine I passed some sort of test.'

'It doesn't sound a very pleasant atmosphere to work in . . .'

'He isn't there much during the week, his wife told me, he's a very busy guy. I doubt if I'll see much of him.'

Karen folded a pair of small pants and picked up a matching shirt. 'I don't know what my kids do with their clothes, I think they have some sort of self-destruct impulse—look at the collar of this, half off!' She began to iron the shirt. 'More sewing—God, I hate sewing! I'll do it while I watch the TV this evening. When do you start working there, then?'

'Tomorrow.' Sasha stopped speaking, catching sight of some framed photographs on the sideboard. One of them was a picture of herself and Philip on their wedding day; her veil had blown across Philip's face, and he was laughing as he put a hand up to brush it away. She felt cold as she picked up the photograph, studying his half-concealed features. His face had been long, slightly Celtic, his bones angular and his jaw pronounced. Light blue eyes, a firm, gentle mouth; he had been a very quiet man, a little stubborn yet always reasonable—that was why he had allowed her parents to talk them into waiting. Philip had seen their point of view. Sasha hadn't: for the first time she wondered if Philip had felt the same driving need for her that she had felt for him. Her emotions had been wild, explosive; Philip had been more mature, he had accepted the waiting period calmly.

Putting down the photograph with a frown, Sasha walked across to the window and looked down into the paved yard behind the shop. Her nephews were playing there; behind them climbed sunflowers which reared towards the sky, their top-heavy heads hanging, dark-eyed, above the children. Staring absently at the small figures below her, Sasha suddenly thought about

Madeleine Fox and began to smile. It was going to be fun looking after her; in spite of the dangerous currents which ran below the surface of that house.

Soon after James Fox arrived home, Sasha had insisted she must get back to London. She had been so uneasy, watching the mockery and insolence in Jake's face as he smiled at Caroline's husband; she had had the strong suspicion that he would have welcomed a violent reaction from James Fox. That had annoyed her so much that she had almost hoped for the same thing; it would have taught Jake Redway a lesson he richly deserved if James had hit him, but she had felt sorry for Caroline. It had seemed a good idea to go and take Jake with her.

'What's going on out there?' Karen asked, coming up behind her to peer suspiciously at her children. 'What were they doing?'

'Nothing, just playing,' Sasha told her. 'They seemed so happy, though, don't you ever envy them? How nice to be five years old again on a sunny day.'

'Romantic,' Karen said with scornful affection, tweaking her ear. 'There's no age more destructive, those innocent little faces are seething with intrigue, jealousy and rage. They quarrel over everything, who's got the biggest apple, the best robot, the most interesting comic. Wait until you have kids, you'll discover things about human nature that will disillusion you for life!'

Sasha took an early train next morning and arrived at the station to find Mrs Fox waiting for her in her car. As she emerged from under green-painted ironwork Sasha saw an arm waving in the small car park and walked over, surprised.

'I was going to take a taxi—this is very kind of you.'

'I had to run James to the station, so I went and did some shopping while I waited for you—no point in taking a taxi when I can ferry you. Hop in.' Caroline Fox opened the passenger door and Sasha slid into the seat, slotting her case into the back of the car.

They drove away down a narrow hill lined with detached houses, a green oasis before they hit the village, which had the air of having sprouted rather than been built deliberately, the houses higgledy-piggledy, all sizes, shapes and periods, nudging each other or detached and standoffish; some in long, hedge-bound gardens, some tiny behind little white-painted picket fences, some in terraces with front doors opening out on to the narrow village street. There were some shops close together, right in the dip of the hill; two public houses, a stone-built church with a high steeple and a village school.

Caroline Fox drove through the village at a snail's pace, behind a milk lorry, keeping up a running commentary on what they passed, waving at other women occasionally, as the car slowed beside them.

'A friendly place,' she told Sasha. 'Really, it is. Of course most of the men are in town all day, at work. Between nine and five this is what you might call a female community, you almost never see a man under sixty-five, except shopkeepers.'

'Is Mrs Carter looking after Madeline?' asked Sasha, and the other woman nodded, turning left at the traffic lights at the end of the village. She put on speed now that she had parted company with the milk lorry and had an empty road in front of her and a moment later they were turning into the gateway of her house.

'It isn't far to the village, you see,' she pointed out as she swung the car round in front of her home. Caroline got out and Sasha did the same, fishing her case out of the back of the car before she followed Caroline into the house. The hall was heavy with the scent of lavender polish, Mrs Carter was standing on a stool at the fireplace, vigorously polishing the mantelshelf above it. On the floor sat Madeleine in pink gingham; a brief cotton dress which showed her matching knickers. She staggered to her feet to meet her mother, who picked her up.

'Say hello to Sasha, darling.'

'Wo,' said Madeleine, mouth bulging.

Caroline put a finger into her pouting lips and winkled out a small doll's head. The plastic had been thoroughly chewed. Caroline put it into her pocket and Madeleine grinned at Sasha.

'Wo.'

'Hallo, Madeleine,' Sasha smiled.

'Lesson number one—you have to watch her, everything goes into her mouth,' Caroline said, laughing.

'Coffee?' asked Mrs Carter, stiffly descending, a gnarled hand on the back of a chair.

'We'd love some,' Caroline said. 'Sasha, come up and deposit your case in your room first. Would you like to unpack right away?'

'It can wait, no hurry.' Sasha followed her up the stairs and laid the case on a chair to look around. 'What lovely flowers!'

'Mrs Carter picked them early this morning—I hope you like flowers in your bedroom, I know some people don't, but I think they make the room smell so nice—you can put them in the bathroom at night if you like.'

Sasha bent over the large green china vase, sniffing. Roses, big plush ones with yellow hearts, their velvety pink and deep red petals just opening; stiff little clusters of Sweet Williams; white carnations and clove-scented ragged pinks, dark blue delphiniums—the massed scents were heady. She straightened, smiling at Caroline.

'I love them. Real flowers are so much nicer, if you know what I mean—bought flowers grown in greenhouses never smell like that.'

Caroline glowed, cheeks flushed, green eyes brilliant. 'I'm so glad you could come here—we can talk theatre, you can't imagine how much I miss it at times and there's nobody to talk to about it, nobody who *understands*. I've made friends here, they're a nice lot in the village, but it's such a different world. When they do go to a theatre they call it seeing a show, as though it was a circus—I think they see actors as clowns.'

'Or performing seals,' Sasha agreed, amused, then thought of Jake Redway. 'Or caged lions,' she added.

'Coffee!' Mrs Carter yelled up the stairs. Caroline turned towards the door. 'Come down when you're ready,' she said, and Sasha followed her.

'I'm ready now, I'm dying for a cup of coffee.'

After lunch that first day Caroline and Madeleine both had a rest upstairs. Sasha helped Mrs Carter with the washing up, then went for a walk around the garden for ten minutes. It was carefully kept, very English; waves of scent from the roses filled the hot afternoon air and even the birds sounded drowsy; perhaps they were taking a siesta too, she thought, as she wandered back towards the house in time to bring Madeleine down. Caroline was asleep, curled up on her bed, a hand under her flushed cheek. Sasha glanced at her from the door, then went downstairs with Madeleine.

'Mrs Fox is asleep,' she told Mrs Carter.

'Well, thank Gawd for that—the trouble I have getting her to snatch an hour's peace you wouldn't believe! She may not look it, but she's as obstinate as a pig over some things.'

'I'll take Madeleine for a walk,' Sasha said. 'If Mrs Fox wakes up tell her I won't be gone too long.'

'Put her bonnet on,' Mrs Carter advised. 'That sun's too hot for her.'

Sasha strapped the little girl into her pushchair, a sunbonnet on her black curls, and fastened the fringed parasol over the chair, then went off along the drive with her at an easy pace. She did not turn towards the village, she turned right and walked along the high hedge, keeping close to the side of the road in case a car came towards them, but no car passed her. The lane was empty and full of the haze of dancing sunlight on the tarmac. Madeleine chattered to herself and Sasha indiscriminately, kicking her white shoes in the air from time to time. Most of what she said was incomprehensible, but from her happy tone she was enjoying their walk. Sasha watched the diving flight of the swallows from one side of the lane to the other and felt strangely happy, herself; there was a drowsy peace about the landscape, about walking slowly with the child, watching the zigzag darting swallows against the blue sky.

They turned back half an hour later and had almost reached the gate when a car swept up behind them and pulled up. Sasha turned to glance back, but Madeleine had already recognised the driver.

'Daddy, Daddy!' she exclaimed, waving. 'Car, car—Daddy!'

'So it is, darling,' Sasha murmured warily as James Fox got out and walked towards them. Madeleine seemed delighted to see him—Sasha was not so enthusiastic!

'Have you been for a walk?' he asked Madeleine, who held up her arms to him. Sasha watched in surprise as he bent and unfastened his daughter to pick her up. This was a totally different man from the one she had met on her last visit; his coldly handsome face softened and warmed as he lifted his daughter into his arms, and kissed her smooth cheek while she patted his face lovingly. 'Want a drive in the car?' he asked Madeleine.

'Car, car,' she said in obvious approval.

James Fox glanced at Sasha. 'Hallo, Miss Lewis. If you'll fold the pushchair up and slip it into the boot, I'll drive you the rest of the way.'

Sasha hurriedly collapsed the pushchair, pushed it and the parasol into the boot and got into the passenger seat with Madeleine on her lap. James Fox drove slowly through the gate and up the drive, the shadows of the trees playing over his austere features.

'Is my wife out?' he asked.

'She was napping on the bed when we left,' Sasha told him, wondering if he was suspicious of his wife's whereabouts or merely being polite. He shot her a look through thick, black lashes and smiled suddenly—giving her a glimpse of charm she had not suspected.

'That's good. She has anaemia, did she tell you? She should be taking her iron pills regularly, but Caro can be awkward—will you keep an eye on her for me?'

'I'll try to,' Sasha said uncertainly; her mind confused by other thoughts, she was happy to make sure Mrs Fox took her iron pills, but she was not playing the spy for him in any other way. Whatever sort of war was going on in this house, she wanted no part of it.

'How long have you known Redway?' he asked.

'Jake?' Sasha felt herself going poppy red and was furious, especially when he looked sideways and noticed the blush. She was so off balance that she found herself stammering: 'He saved my life years ago when . . .' She stopped abruptly, even more flushed. What on earth had made her blurt that out?

The car had pulled up outside the house, James Fox turned to watch her, his arm along the wheel, his face shrewdly observant. Those grey eyes were penetrating, they seemed to look right through your head. She found him one of the most alarming and disturbing men she had ever met; he seemed able to see what you were thinking, but she hadn't got a clue what was going on inside his head.

'Do you see much of him?'

'I hadn't set eyes on him since . . .' Sasha found herself starting off again in a sentence she found too revealing to finish, she bit her lower lip, angry. He somehow managed to startle truths out of her when she usually found it easy to conceal her thoughts. His face was far too clever; perceptive, remote, watching you from a distance but coolly intelligent. 'I hardly know him,' she finished. Did he imagine she was one of Jake Redway's women? She did not want him to think that, the very idea annoyed her.

'He isn't an easy man to know,' James Fox murmured, and got out of the car, leaving her wondering what he meant by that.

The summer weather continued without a break, day after day, and Sasha found herself settling into a routine imposed as much by the weather as by herself or Caroline. 'While it's so fine Madeleine should have plenty of fresh air,' Caro had decided, and each day they spent most of the daylight hours either in the garden, or walking in the countryside. So much sun and exercise made both Caro and her daughter fall asleep easily. Sasha would have time on her hands during the afternoon and would take a book and read on the lawn, in her bikini, killing two birds with one stone: sunbathing and making her way through a lot of books she had been meaning to read for years but hadn't got around to opening.

She saw little of James Fox, which was a relief. He was working very hard on a case which kept him in London until late in the evening. Sasha went to bed early and he had always gone before she got up. Caroline was not the sort of woman who talks about her private life; she never breathed a word to Sasha about either Jake or her husband, and Sasha was only too pleased to follow suit. She liked Caroline more each day; the other woman was warm, impulsive, lively, it was easy to like her. James Fox was a very different kettle of fish, Sasha didn't know quite what she thought of him, but she was very wary of offending or irritating him. His cold frown made her very nervous.

He arrived home early one afternoon, during Sasha's second week with them, just as Caro was shepherding Madeleine into the house for her tea. James Fox swung his daughter, shrieking with laughter, up on to his shoulder. 'What have you been up to?' he demanded, and Caro protested: 'Don't frighten her with your court voice, James!' He looked down at his wife, his brows rising, and Sasha saw Caro bite her lower lip.

The phone rang at that moment. 'I'll get it,' said Sasha, relieved to get away. The last voice she expected to hear on the other end was that of Jake Redway. Her face altered, stiffening. 'Did you want Mrs Fox?' She couldn't keep the ice out of her voice, and Jake laughed drily.

'No, I rang to ask if you'd like to go to the first night of the new Gerrard play.'

She was torn by conflicting impulses; her first instinct to tell him coldly no, thank you, and ring off, but other feelings following hot on the heels of that one, a strong wish to see the play since Alex Gerrard was a writer she admired, and an even stronger interest because she knew one of the actors, a very successful guy who had auditioned her when she first applied for her drama school and who had several times taken her out during her years there.

Her long silence irritated Jake Redway. 'Hallo? Are you still there?' he asked impatiently.

'Yes, sorry, I was thinking,' she said huskily. 'It's very kind of you.'

'Do you want to come or not?'

Why had he asked? she wondered, knowing he could not want her company that much. He hadn't shown the slightest personal interest in her. This must be some ploy to do with Caro Fox, and again she felt like refusing, but the bait he was dangling in front of her was very tempting. She'd love to see that play, first nights were exhilarating.

'Thank you,' she began again, still uncertainly, and he interrupted, speaking rapidly.

'Fine, then I'll pick you up tomorrow night at four-thirty, we'll have a little supper before the curtain goes up. See you tomorrow.'

'Mr Redway——' she tried to say, and then the phone clicked. He had hung up. She put the phone down slowly. It was obvious why he had invited her, it gave him an excuse to drive down here tomorrow afternoon and see Caroline, all under cover of seeing Sasha. She stood, frowning, for a moment, angry with him, then went out, and Caroline was still standing in the hall with her husband and Madeleine. They looked round, and Sasha gave them an uneasy smile.

'Good news?' Caroline looked almost excitedly at her, as if sharing the prospect of a job, entering into Sasha's feelings, imagining herself in Sasha's place.

'It was Jake—he invited me to the Alex Gerrard first night.' Sasha couldn't make her voice enthusiastic, although she tried, it merely came out as flat and phoney. She saw a flicker of feeling in the other woman's face, passing over it like a ripple over still water, so quickly that it had gone before she could identify it.

James Fox's eyes narrowed, but when Sasha looked into those eyes she found them suddenly blank, his features wooden—but wasn't that, in itself, a sort of betrayal? The careful emptiness of expression could only mean that he was hiding something, but this was a clever man; whatever he was concealing left no clues on the surface, she knew she wouldn't be able to pierce that calm mask. She might guess at what he was thinking because of what she knew from other sources, but James Fox wouldn't give anything away. He must be a terrific poker player, she wouldn't sit down to play against him.

He wasn't the only one hiding something. Caroline was chattering away about the Gerrard play. 'Lucky you, it's supposed to be his best so far, you'll have a great evening.' But what was she hiding? What was it that had flashed so briefly across her face—jealousy, surprise, anger? Or had it been the amused comprehension of someone watching someone else being taken in by a trick they've helped set up?

Charming, Sasha thought: delightful to be used and smiled at behind your back, what nice people. At least she had no difficulties deciphering her own emotions, she was damned mad, anger was making her skin prickle, she was sweating with something like embarrassment, except that it was closer to humiliated rage. Did the two of them think she was some dumb bunny who had hopped in off the green meadows and didn't know her nose from her tail? What a nerve, if they thought . . .

'You'd better stay in London afterwards,' said James Fox, breaking into her incoherent thoughts. 'You won't want to drive back here at that hour.' He walked away, carrying his daughter, and Caroline smiled at Sasha.

'He's right, much better spend the night at your flat.'

For some reason Sasha was in a mood to break things, to hit back. She was an actress, too; she could hide how she felt and put on a false front. She smiled gaily. 'I'm sure that was Jake's intention!' Ambiguous, but carefully phrased.

Caroline's face set in lines of surprise; eyes wide, lips parted on a silent gasp. She took the meaning Sasha had intended her to take, and before she could say any more Sasha had walked past. If she *was* Jake's lover, Caroline was going to ask herself how far Jake would go in using Sasha as a front for their affair. Jake Redway notoriously had a way with women; his name was always being mentioned with that of some pretty actress or society lady, he was hardly a famous celibate, nor obviously did he have that many scruples to his name, or he wouldn't be cheerfully prepared to make use of someone in this way. Where would he draw the line? Would he merely throw up a smokescreen of dating Sasha, or would he go so far as to try to talk her into bed in order to give his lie some validity?

After all, if he was to convince James Fox he had, first, to convince Sasha that she was his object, rather than Caroline. Sasha's face stiffened in chilly distaste. He could think again, he wasn't sweet-talking her into his bed just to hide his affair with another woman, as far as she was concerned he was as irresistible as an old sock. Let him try to lay one finger on her and she'd belt him so hard he wouldn't talk for a month! Any girl dim enough to be taken in by his brand of sexy charm would have to be off her trolley for life and deserve everything she got. It was time someone told Jake Redway in categoric terms exactly what he was—and Sasha was the girl to do it!

By the time Jake arrived next afternoon she was still in a temper, but she was disguising it with grim determination, partly because Caroline was making a very good job of being cheerful and apparently unconcerned and Sasha wasn't going to be runner-up in the award for best actress of the year, no way. If Caroline could smile and talk as if everything was just fine in her world, so could Sasha. She found herself watching Caroline all the time, speculating about her feelings behind that light smile, hurriedly smiling back if their eyes met, and angrily recognised that they were in competition, each vying to show how rosy the world looked to them. The realisation didn't please Sasha: she didn't want to be in competition with Caroline Fox, either to prove her acting ability or to get Jake Redway, particularly not the latter.

His car shot up the drive just after four o'clock. Sasha had expected him to arrive earlier than he had promised, he would want to see Caroline and if he got there early he could be reasonably certain that Sasha would be dressing upstairs. He was right, she was, but she heard the roar of his engine and looked at herself in the mirror, teeth tight. She should have placed a bet with the local bookmaker, she'd have won handsomely. She was beginning to anticipate his every move. He might think he was as clever as a wagonload of monkeys, but once you understood the motivation it was easy to predict a behaviour pattern.

She had chosen her dress intentionally, a dramatic flame-red taffeta, with a low scooped neckline, tiny puff sleeves of patterned lace and a full, layered skirt which rustled and swished as she walked. Around her throat she clipped a heavy bronze-gold necklet whose dull sheen complemented the colour of the dress, emphasised the smooth tan she had acquired over the last few weeks. She brushed soft blue along her lids, delicately applied mascara to her long eyelashes, glossed her lips in a shade that matched the dress. Her hair had been newly washed, it curled around her face in a casual frame.

As she surveyed her own reflection her mouth twisted wryly. Seen from the outside she could be dressing to attract Jake Redway, you would have to get inside her head to know that she was dressing for the sake of her own ego. She might despise the man, she might be as angry as hell with him, but no woman likes to be used the way Jake Redway was using her; she meant to tell him so at the first opportunity, but she was going to do so from a position of strength. He wasn't going to have a chance to imply that she was jealous of Caroline—Sasha was going to look just as good as she could before she stuck her neck out and accused him, he wasn't smiling behind her back and thinking that she had an inferiority complex.

She was going into battle fully-armed and confident.

She went downstairs in a drift of expensive perfume, she had used up the last drops in a bottle which Billy had given her for Christmas. As she reached the foot of the stairs she heard low, intimate voices in the sitting-room and paused, frowning.

Caroline laughed huskily and said something too quietly for Sasha to catch the words.

'Caro, you idiot!' Jake said in a deep, warm tone, and Sasha heard so much in his voice that she had to force herself to walk forward. She didn't want to join them, she didn't want to see their faces, their voices said it all, only lovers murmur like that to each other—and as she opened the door she felt as out of place and conspicuous as an elephant in a tea-shop, but she could not bear to hear any more, it was too painfully personal.

They were standing near the window, close together, not touching, but something in the posture of their bodies betraying to her an involuntary drift towards each other, consciously restrained. They were not touching because they dared not, she thought. The room was sunlit, yet to her it seemed shadowy, the two at the window darker shadows, outlined against the light beyond the window. She did not see their faces, they were looking outwards, not towards her, and for a strange second she did not think of them as Jake and Caroline, she saw only two nameless lovers, trapped in pain. She felt she had seen this before, she was looking into the past or the future; this moment was not real, it was projected from elsewhere.

Then they turned and the experience broke up into real life, happening now. 'What a fantastic dress, it's gorgeous!' Caroline exclaimed. 'Doesn't she look marvellous, Jake?'

'All she needs is a rose between her teeth,' said Jake, laughing. 'If you're expecting me to dance flamenco with you, you're going to be disappointed.'

'I'm sure I am,' said Sasha with an angry flicker of derision, and his bright blue eyes widened and stared, his black brows rose sharply at her intonation, at the double meaning behind it.

'If you're going to have supper first, you'd better rush,' said Caroline, seeming unaware of the implication of what she had said.

Sasha turned with a rustle of skirts, her head high, and felt Jake walking just behind her. His car was parked outside, he slid Sasha into the passenger seat. She jerked her arm away almost as soon as he had touched it and again he looked at her speculatively.

'Have a wonderful time, you can tell me all about it tomorrow,' Caroline called through the open window.

Smiling stiffly, Sasha waved as the car drove off through the gates. Jake turned into the road beyond, then settled down to a steady sixty miles an hour before he asked without looking at her: 'Is something wrong?'

Sasha's mind reverberated with all the things she wanted to say to him, she felt like the scene of a railway crash; everything jaggedly in confusion and noisy chaos.

CHAPTER FIVE

WHEN she didn't answer, he turned and gave her a quizzical look, his mouth curling at the edges. 'Are you in one of your moods?' he asked as casually and with as much familiarity as though they had known each other for years. 'Snap out of it pronto. Temperament doesn't impress me, it's just a bind. Only actors of the first rank can afford displays of temperament, and even then they're being self-indulgent and they know it; with them it's often a safety valve, if it doesn't blow they could go screaming right over the top. You don't come into that category.' He laughed suddenly, blue eyes mocking. 'Yet,' he added in heavy sarcasm.

'But you do,' Sasha supplied for him. 'Of course.' Even as she flung the jibe at him she knew she was being unjust; he had no reputation for being a temperamental actor, if anything his reputation was for taking everything he did too lightly, and that included himself as an actor, he was not one of those actors who expect rose petals showered on their heads every time they appear in public.

He seemed indifferent to the little sneer, he just laughed and said softly: 'Bitch.'

Inside Sasha's head her vision of him shifted again, for the third time since she met him in the dressing-room on the last night of her play. The wryly amused retort made him likeable, human.

She found herself smiling, and he smiled back at her.

He drove on, leaning forward to switch on a tape which was already slotted into the tape deck at the base of the dashboard. 'Do you like Elkie Brooks?' he asked as the singer's husky voice breathed out into the car.

'Yes,' said Sasha, half relieved by the music, half irritated by what had preceded it. It was not part of her game plan for her to find herself liking the man; she had come out intending to straighten him out about a few things and already he had sidestepped neatly, altering the whole atmosphere. How had he done it? that was what she wanted to know. She watched him through her lashes, infuriated, realising that she had been upstaged by a superior technique. Jake Redway was walking away with the show and she wasn't stopping him.

'Caro tells me that Madeleine has taken to you like a duck to water,' he remarked.

'It's mutual, I'm enjoying looking at her.' That much she could be frank about. Madeleine was all joy, Sasha got great fun out of playing with her and looking after her. Every time she looked at the little girl she ached for her, remembering the adult confusion which was raging over Madeleine's small head. How could Caroline risk her daughter's happiness like this? Anyone with half an eye could see that Madeleine adored her father and he thought the sun shone out of her. It would be tragic if anything parted them. If Caroline was deeply in love with Jake Redway it was very sad, Sasha could sympathise, you couldn't help your own emotions, but the barbed triangle which was Caroline's way of dealing with the situation could only end in disaster for everyone concerned. The three adults might in time weather the storm, but who knew what it would do to Madeleine?

She was silent as they drove towards London in the sunny afternoon, her face sombre, and Jake glanced at her again a short time later. She felt his glance but didn't look up, heard him draw a breath and start to speak, but did not anticipate what he actually said.

'How old were you when you got married?'

The shock of the question held her frozen for a few seconds. It was a simple enough question, anyone might have asked it casually if they had known about her marriage, there was no reason why she should find it so painful just because it came from Jake Redway. Except, of course, that she would always associate him with her husband's death.

'Twenty,' she said at last, and felt his deep attention fixed on her, there had, after all, been nothing casual about the question, it had been a steely probe inserted into her mind with the calculation of a surgeon looking for a cancer. Sasha knew it, felt intuitively a desire not to answer. Why should she gratify Jake Redway's neutral curiosity about her past when she had avoided such curiosity even when it came from people who loved her, like Billy or Karen? If she did not talk about her husband or her marriage it was because it hurt too much, Billy and Karen understood that, but apparently Jake Redway felt no such compunction. When she shrank from the pain of remembering, he merely wanted to lay bare the reasons why, and she resented his curiosity.

'Very young,' he commented.

She didn't bother to reply.

'How long had you known him?'

Sasha shifted angrily, her face tense. 'I don't want to talk about it.' She couldn't make the refusal sound polite, it came out almost hoarsely, which was in itself betraying. She would have preferred to sound icily calm.

'That's obvious, but why? I can understand why you wouldn't have wanted to talk about him at first, but after all this time . . .'

'I don't want to be rude . . .' Sasha broke in fiercely, and he swung his head again to stare at her.

'Then don't be!'

'Don't force me to, I've told you I prefer not to discuss my private life, just stay off the subject.'

'You *should* talk about your marriage,' he said, the sun shining into his blue eyes and too dazzling for her to look at him any more. She turned and stared at the road and Jake said quietly: 'You know you should talk about him—it helps. It's dangerous to repress things.'

'Don't give me that psychological claptrap about repression; it always leads on to the suggestion that a little hygienic sex would make the world a brighter place.'

'Don't you ever think of anything else?' Jake drawled, and she flushed hotly.

'I didn't raise the subject.'

'Well, I certainly didn't,' he retorted. 'The way I remember it, I was talking about your marriage— it was you who dragged sex into the discussion, but then you always do, whatever the subject I'm talking about you start accusing me of wanting to go to bed with you.'

Sasha opened her mouth; then, speechless, shut it again. How did he do it? For the second time he had performed a mental somersault, leaving her standing there struck dumb, and now she would be very inhibited about accusing him of using her to cover an affair with Caroline Fox. He would coolly turn round and mock her; repeat what he had just said, that whatever the subject he was discussing she always brought it round to sex. Maybe he was right, that hadn't occurred to her until now. Was her imagination working overtime? Was his relationship with Caroline simply that of very old, very close friends? But then why had he invited her to this play? Was he interested in her? She frowned impatiently, pushing that idea away. Jake Redway was a smooth operator, he confused the eye with his clever tricks with words, juggling with them so deftly that your gaze could not move fast enough to follow and pinpoint where the exchange had taken place.

'No comeback?' he mocked, and she felt her face grow hotter. The music had ended, so she leaned forward and pulled out the tape, turned it and re-inserted it. They both listened in silence after that. Sasha felt silence was safer and perhaps Jake felt the same, for he made no attempt to talk again until they were in the centre of London and he began to mutter under his breath as he looked for somewhere to park.

'Traffic gets worse every day—God, London's a madhouse, I should have parked further out and taken a taxi.'

By the time he had parked and they had looked at the time, it was too late to have supper before the performance. They settled for a drink, instead, after a polite debate on the pavement outside a pub close to the theatre. There were white-painted iron tables outside it, with customers seated there drinking and watching the passers-by. A couple got up and wandered off, Sasha quickly sat down at their vacated table before anyone else could take it, while Jake went inside the pub to get their drinks.

He came back five minutes later with a tray; a glass of ale for him and a Martini for her, a packet of crisps and a bag of peanuts. Some people at the next table stared, whispered to each other. Jake sat down and handed Sasha her glass. A thin little blonde from the next table came over, a book in her hand, and Jake turned and looked at her blankly.

'Mr Redway?' The girl wasn't quite certain, Sasha saw that, her voice was hesitant and she was peering at Jake feature by feature.

'Sorry?' he said, miming bafflement.

'It's Jake Redway, isn't it? You are, aren't you?'

'Yes, and this is Elizabeth Taylor,' said Jake, grinning and picking up his beer, drinking almost half of it in one swallow. 'Sorry, darling, this isn't your big day, I'm afraid,' he added as he put down the glass.

The girl backed, mumbling, very pink. 'Oh, sorry, you look like him, didn't anyone tell you, but I thought it couldn't really be—what would Jake Redway be doing drinking beer outside a London pub like anybody else?'

'What indeed?' Sasha murmured softly as the girl fled back to her friends, who giggled and stared and then lost interest, returning to their noisy argument about who was paying for the drinks.

Jake grimaced at her covertly. 'It's so long since I was in London I'd begun to feel invisible—people don't expect to see you, they walk past without a second look, or if they do notice you they think you're just a double. I can't go out in the streets in the States any more, it was great to be home and feel anonymous.'

'The price of fame,' Sasha said with a sting of aggression. 'Spare me the stuff about it being tough at the top, please, I haven't got my box of Kleenex handy.'

'You wasp,' he said, eyes sharp, and she laughed, half sorry, because she could imagine what a bore it must be to be unable to relax in public.

'You don't like me, do you?' he challenged, his black brows heavy above his eyes, and she was taken by surprise, staring back, then flushing. 'I'm on your hit list because of the way we met,' he added. 'Not that I expect a woman to be purely rational, but aren't you being a little unfair? What do you want me to do? Apologise for saving your life when you didn't want it saved? Believe me, next time I see a woman drowning I'll wait until she gives me permission to pull her out of the sea, I won't stick my neck out again.'

Unsteadily she put her glass down on the table and some of the golden liquid spilled. She touched it with one long finger, her head bent, feeling guilty.

'I wish I could explain—you make me sound crazy.'

'That's how it looks to me, darling,' he said brusquely.

'We'd been married such a short time, they made us wait two years—two whole years I lost. I think it was that that hurt so much, the thought of all the time we'd wasted when we could have been together.' Her voice broke, the salt taste of pain in her mouth, she breathed carefully because she couldn't cry here, in public, with people walking past and seeing her, and Jake Redway watching her across the table with those narrowed, hard blue eyes. Pain was something she had lived with ever since that day, familiar to her as her own skin, she drew it on at night as she fell asleep and lay with it all through the dark hours. It was there when she woke up, wrenched from Philip's arms by the intrusive light.

Jake put a hand across the table to touch her and she jerked away, involuntarily, stiffening, as if his skin would burn if it brushed her. She heard him draw breath sharply and regretted the movement.

'Sorry, I didn't mean . . .'

'I know what you meant,' he said, snapping the words between his teeth like taut thread. 'You have a problem, Miss Lewis, but I'm not a psychologist, I can't solve it for you, I only know that I'm rather sick of being blamed for something which is not my fault. A time of mourning should only go on so long—after three years you ought to have got over the grief.' He saw her face, the protest in her eyes, and before she could say anything went on roughly: 'I'm not saying you should forget him, obviously you'll never do that, but I am saying that you aren't accepting what happened, you haven't admitted to yourself that he's dead and you're not, you're still angry about it, which means you're refusing to face it, and while you won't face it, you're still locked into the past, which isn't a healthy situation.' He finished his beer while Sasha sat staring at her own barely touched glass.

He was right, of course; she couldn't deny that. Philip would probably have been the first to tell her to put the past behind her. He had always been a man who used his common sense; that was why he had accepted their long engagement without anger, while Sasha had raged with frustration. Philip had loved her, of course, but while her own emotions had been chaotic, passionate, violent, Philip's love had been quiet and gentle; a steady rock on which she had leant with a sense of peace.

'Ready?' Jake asked shortly, getting up, and she followed him into the theatre. They had excellent seats in the front row and Sasha knew her friend in the cast had spotted her early on, because he looked her way several times. When the curtain came down after the first act, Jake asked: 'Do we go out or stay here?'

'Up to you,' she said, because she was in no danger of being recognised and surrounded by excited fans.

'I don't know about you, but I need a drink,' said Jake, getting up in a fluid movement which suddenly riveted her eyes on him. He was wearing a smoothly tailored dark suit; it looked much too good on his lean body, made her far too aware of his deep chest, slim hips and long legs. Jake had the sort of looks which come from an awareness of sexuality; an impression of masculinity in every move he made, every word he spoke in that deep, husky voice. There was the implicit hint of violence behind his strong face and those dark blue, dangerously sexy eyes.

'Well, are you coming?' he asked, looking down at her. Then his eyes narrowed, as though he saw something betraying in her face, and she found herself suddenly very hot, breathing unevenly.

She stumbled to her feet, literally, almost falling, and he caught her, an arm around her waist. She felt it intensely as it touched her, his body warmth meeting her own through the layers of cloth separating them. Her mind jerked, like a train leaping the tracks, she felt a series of emotions one after the other, colliding and crashing inside her: a powerful urge to touch him, a weakness deep inside her which made her flesh dissolve in appalling longing, a need which had no real connection with the man holding her but which was born of long frustration and a natural physical hunger, and then immediately on the heels of all that a burning anger with herself for having let such feelings loose.

She had not even been conscious of Jake Redway, the man himself: only of her own desire, a desire she bitterly repudiated as soon as she had recognised it.

She pushed him away, straightened and walked on without looking round. It had all happened too fast, nobody had noticed, everyone was streaming out to get to the bar and their drink. All around her people talked and laughed and jostled. Sasha was shaky and sick—how could she have felt like that? She was rigid with embarrassment. Had he noticed? Surely he couldn't have guessed, she hadn't looked up at him, he couldn't have read anything in her face. But if he had! If they had been alone somewhere and he had picked up what was happening inside her? What might have happened then? The very idea of sleeping with him without feeling anything but that terrible need horrified her. It would diminish her idea of herself to take a man simply because he was a man and alive and could end a sexual hunger she bitterly wished she did not feel.

'Another Martini?' he asked at her shoulder, and she jumped visibly.

'Oh, yes, thanks,' she stammered.

Jake gave her a hard stare. 'One day soon someone is going to prove to you that you're a human being like everyone else,' he said, then turned and walked to the bar.

People did recognise him, she saw them look twice, then hurriedly pretend not to have noticed him. More than that, she noticed that Jake's face was different; he didn't look aside or at anyone he passed, he seemed to walk inside a forcefield which held everyone at bay; he was aware of them but silently willing them to ignore him, and they picked up that warning and stayed clear.

They finished the drinks, talking about the play. It was a neutral subject, and they became quite excited as their views clashed. It was a surprise when the bell rang and people started moving back into the auditorium.

The second half was even better than the first, it built to a few moments of powerful emotion; you could hear a pin drop, people tried not to breathe too loudly in case they missed a word. When the curtain came down a tiny silence held them all before a storm of applause broke out.

Sasha felt the hair on the back of her neck

prickling; excitement always brought her close to tears, which embarrassed her in public, and she blinked hard to keep them back.

The curtain came up, the cast began to take their bows. Sasha's friend glanced down at her, smiling ecstatically. As he bowed he mouthed in her direction: 'Come round.' She read his lips and as he straightened, nodded

When the curtain came down for the last time and everyone started shuffling out she turned to Jake to start: 'I've been invited to . . .'

'I know,' he said drily. 'I can lipread too.'

'I can take a taxi home if you want to go,' she said quickly. She would much rather he did that, she wanted to go back stage and talk to the cast, she was strung up and high on the adrenalin of the performance and she wanted to talk, but she would enjoy herself much more if Jake wasn't there. He inhibited her; when he was around she felt too conscious of herself.

'I'm in no hurry. You're staying in London tonight, aren't you? Why don't we go round, congratulate your friend and then have some supper?' He looked at her, reading her expression, his mocking eyes challenging her. 'Or can't you stand any more of my company?' Sasha flushed at that direct and deliberate question and realised that he had made it impossible for her to say no, which had, of course, been his intention.

'Thank you,' she said through her teeth, following the throng of people on their way to the exit. Jake's shoulder touched hers as they were jostled; she felt the light pressure with a strange sense of panic which she couldn't explain.

'How long have you known Peter Temple?' he asked.

'Ages,' she said tersely.

He considered her. 'Secretive, aren't you? You're not quite with us all; you're always miles away.' He paused, watching her averted face. 'Or years away,' he added drily. 'With a dead man.' Sasha stiffened at that, her eyes lowered.

'What was he like? He must have been something special for you to go on missing him all this time—tell me about him, what sort of guy was he?'

'Why do you keep asking me questions you must know I don't want to answer?' she broke out angrily, and part of her anger came from realising how little she had really known about Philip. She had been too young to see anyone else clearly; she hadn't seen herself with any depth of clarity, how could she have understood anyone else? She had loved Philip with an intensity which she saw now had come from first love; from the very fact that she did not understand him, he had been the unknown, the mysterious, the other sex, and the fact that her parents had refused to let them get married had made him all the more desirable to her.

'If you'd talked about him more in the past, maybe you wouldn't be so locked up now,' Jake drawled, and she wondered how close he came to the truth.

'Was he good-looking?' Jake insisted, and she shook her head. Philip had been attractive, his smile when it came had been warm and gentle, lighting his whole face, but it had been his quiet strength which had drawn her, not his looks.

'How long had you been married?' Jake asked casually, and her breath caught in raw agony. She was afraid to answer in case she lost control; she had to hide her feelings, it was the only way she could cope with them. That was what she had learnt as she lived through the pain of Philip's death; her emotions had been so intense that she could only bear them if she forced them out of sight.

They had halted at the stage door; a small crowd were jostling around it, under the yellow glare of a street lamp. The light fell on her face, Jake watched her, searching her eyes. 'How long had you been married?' he repeated, and she suddenly resented him so much that she threw the truth at him in a harsh voice.

'We were on our honeymoon.' After waiting for two years with mounting impatience and need, they had married only to be parted again within days; and this time for ever. The shock had been more than Sasha could stand; only numb withdrawal could make it possible to go on living without him. She had needed Philip's calm strength so much, looking back she did not know how she had found the courage to bear his death at all.

Jake's eyes hardened and darkened, all pupil, black and glittering and angry. Why was he angry? she wondered vaguely, looking down. He pushed her through the crowd and the doorman looked at him hard, then smiled. 'Evening, Mr Redway.' Sasha heard the excited murmur of the fans, then she was thrust through the stage door, as though she had behaved badly, Jake wanted to smack her. She wasn't sure what she had expected, but it

wasn't this impatient, hustling irritation. Or was
he angry with himself for having forced her to tell
him? Without a word he propelled her down the
corridor, his fingers tight around her arm, hurting
her; but with that frown on his face Sasha did not
dare to complain.

There was a crowd of people in Peter's dressing-
room, but Peter saw them hovering at the door
and waved excitedly. 'Get a glass, come on in . . .'
He was very flushed and held a glass of
champagne; everyone seemed to have a glass of
champagne and Sasha felt them all staring at Jake.
Peter was excited to have him there; the whole
room was full of the buzz of a company which
knows it has a big success it hasn't expected. The
audience had gone crazy; everything had worked,
play, cast, direction, it was going to be the biggest
hit Alex Gerrard had ever had. Peter had never
been in a smash hit before; he was walking on his
head.

Hugging Sasha, he whispered: 'How long have
you been making it with Redway? Darling, you
might have told an old buddy! Holding out on
me—not nice!'

'We're not making it,' protested Sasha, going
scarlet.

'Come off it, I wasn't born yesterday! I'm an old
pal, don't try to kid me. He came to see you in
your play, didn't he? On the last night? Adrian
told me.'

'He came to see Maggie!'

Peter pretended to look around. 'So—where's
Maggie tonight?' he mocked, grinning.

He wasn't the only one to make remarks like
that, Sasha met with a lot of teasing curiosity. She

had lost Jake in the confusion; she talked to people, rarely tasting her champagne, which had gone flat and warm, fending off questions which were too embarrassing and wishing she could go soon. Once she bumped into somebody and, turning to mutter: 'Sorry!' found herself meeting Jake's eyes. He smiled at her, his black lashes flicking along his cheeks in an intimate little wink, as though he had overheard some of the questions being jabbed into her. Sasha hurriedly turned away to find herself facing amused eyes; everyone around them had seen that look Jake had given her and had drawn their own conclusions.

In their business, such fascinating gossip spread like wildfire, she knew that by tomorrow morning it would be all over London that she was Jake Redway's latest conquest. Sasha wasn't flattered; there had been so many, who wanted to be one of a crowd? She did find it surprising, though, that she was suddenly very popular, everyone wanted to talk to her. She was surrounded by smiles all the time and it didn't take long for it to dawn on her—someone who was sleeping with an actor with Jake's influence and power was possibly powerful herself; she could influence him, persuade him to get parts for herself and her friends. Sasha had, until now, been an unknown actress with one small part in a short run to her name—from the way she was being treated at this moment she might have been an internationally famous star. As it sank in, she felt sick; then angry. She wanted to leave before she started losing her temper.

Her eyes moved through the throng, searching for Jake, who had moved away to talk to someone else. 'I must go, Peter,' she said. 'We're having supper somewhere—sorry, we can't come on to your party.' It had started, already, anyway; from the look of this tiny dressing-room, crowded to the doors, it would be ages before they moved on to their party. Jake glanced over her way and she waved. He nodded, said something to the group he was with and began to move towards her.

Peter put his arms round her and kissed her lingeringly. Sasha was too taken aback to react, but she was blazingly angry; she knew at once that Peter had done it deliberately, his eyes held mischief as he stood away.

'Wonderful to see you, darling—I'll give you a ring tomorrow.'

Jake joined them and Peter gave him a faintly malicious smile. 'You don't mind, do you? An old buddy's privilege—Sasha and I go way back.'

Jake looked at him consideringly, blue eyes lazily ironic. 'Don't push your luck, chum—no make-up in this world will hide a broken nose.' He put his arm round Sasha and steered her towards the door. She felt everyone staring after them, avid curiosity in their eyes. The whispers became open chatter as they walked out.

Sasha was shaking, with rage not nerves. She was too angry to say anything to Jake, anything she did say would be so violent she might say more than she meant. She did not want to get into a bitter argument with him in public. Enough damage had been done that evening.

'You're dangerously quiet,' Jake observed as he hailed a taxi, across the road from the theatre. 'We'll take a taxi to the Café Royal, have supper and take a taxi back to pick up my car—no point in moving it at this hour, I'll never find a parking place around Piccadilly.'

A taxi screeched to a halt beside them and she climbed into the back of it. Only as they drove away did she remember that she had intended to ask him to drive her straight to her flat. Turning to him she said in a low voice: 'I want to go home now, please, I don't want to go to the Café Royal.' That was a very public place to be seen with him, they might as well spell it out in neon lights in Piccadilly itself.

'Don't be absurd,' he said. 'You must be starving, you haven't eaten all evening. The champagne will give you a rotten head tomorrow if you don't eat now.'

'I want to go home,' she muttered, afraid of the taxi driver overhearing. She knew the man had recognised Jake, he was watching them in his mirror.

Traffic was still heavy, although it was almost midnight now, Shaftesbury Avenue was jammed with cars nose to tail as they crawled along towards Piccadilly. The taxi moved along jerkily and Sasha clung to the seat with both hands to prevent being shot off on to the floor. She felt Jake watching her and glanced round. A speculative mockery gleamed in his blue eyes.

'We agreed we would have supper after the play, why the change of mind?'

'I don't like being talked about,' Sasha muttered, her voice impeded by the pressure of all the angry things she wanted to say and did not dare voice.

His black brows rose. 'What's that supposed to mean? Don't talk in riddles.'

She lowered her voice, leaning back with her shoulder touching his. 'Don't tell me you didn't notice, didn't realise what they were all thinking . . .'

He laughed and she felt rage flaring inside her. He thought it was funny, he had picked up what they were all thinking, but it hadn't bothered him, he had been amused. He was amused now, looking at her with wicked laughter.

'Who cares what they think?' It didn't mean a thing to him, he was used to being talked about, it was water off a duck's back to him.

'I care,' she said furiously. 'It isn't true, and I don't like being labelled as your latest sleeping partner!'

He considered her drily. 'Which order do I take that in?'

She stared back, baffled. 'What?'

'Which comes first—the fact that you don't like being labelled as my girl-friend or that it isn't true?'

Her flushed cheeks deepened in colour, her eyes flashed. 'Very clever! As it's never going to be true you can take it in any order you like.'

'Don't coat-trail,' he drawled. 'Unless you're quite sure you want your coat pounced on.'

Sasha hissed back: 'Try pouncing on me, Mr Redway, and I'll knock your teeth down your throat!'

He sat up, staring at her intently. 'My God, I believe you would,' he said, and laughed again, then said: 'Look, I'm sorry if they all got the wrong impression, nothing I said or did could have given them the idea—you mustn't worry about it, gossip soon gets forgotten. I've lost count of the number of women I'm supposed to have slept with—but you can take my word for it, it vastly over-estimates my love life. I'm a working actor, I'm not a super-stud; most evenings after a day's work in the studios or on location I just crawl into bed with tomorrow's script and try to learn my lines before I get some sleep. The last thing on my mind is sex. But that doesn't make good copy, journalists like a redhot story and it doesn't bother me if they invent one.'

'It will bother me,' Sasha told him.

He sighed. 'I'll deny it if anyone asks me pointblank, I promise you.'

'Do you really think they'll believe you? I tried telling Peter and his friends that it wasn't true, they just laughed and asked who I thought I was kidding.'

The taxi had pulled up at the Café Royal. Jake glanced out of the window, then said to Sasha: 'Look, I don't know about you, but I'm very hungry and it seems stupid not to eat now we're here.'

The taxi driver had leaned over to open their door. Sasha thought rapidly, frowning. He was right, it was stupid, and she was ravenous. She climbed out on to the pavement, Jake paid the driver and they walked towards the entrance.

'It really won't make any difference to the situation whether you go home or have supper here,' Jake pointed out rationally, and she nodded. A little flurry of summer wind blew her taffeta skirts upwards, she held them down with both hands, and Jake watched, grinning.

She laughed back, shaking off her mood of irritated distaste. He was right, it hadn't been his fault that everyone had jumped to the wrong conclusion, and it wasn't every night she got to eat at such a swish place, so she might as well make the most of it while she was here. By next month she might be eating baked beans on toast and feeling grateful to have that much.

'Been here before?' Jake asked as they were shown to their table, and she shook her head, looking around with fascination. She saw several faces she recognised among the other customers and could visualise many others, even more famous, from the past; writers and artists and theatre people who had loved to frequent the restaurant, whose red plush and ornate period décor was so famous.

She browsed through the menu at leisure while Jake watched her, leaning back with an indulgent expression, as though she were a child he was treating. At last she decided on what she would eat and Jake ordered. Over their first course they discussed the play, over the second they wandered on to an enthralling game of swapping famous performances each had seen, finding some in common from more recent years. When Jake rhapsodied about a Gielgud production of *Much Ado About Nothing* Sasha laughed and said: 'I wasn't even born then.'

Jake grimaced wryly, half sulky. 'Don't rub it in—I was still in short trousers, myself, I'm not that old.'

'Late thirties?' guessed Sasha. He stared at her, brows meeting.

'Early,' he said. 'Thirty four to be precise—want to see my birth certificate?' Although he was smiling his eyes were not pleased, they held an irritable glitter. He leaned over to fill her wine glass and she was so taken aback by his offended eyes that she picked up the glass and drank more of the wine which she had been carefully ignoring. She did not want to get drunk, Jake Redway was not the type of man who refused to take advantage of such a situation. She didn't trust him further than she could see him.

After that she set herself out to charm him back into a good humour; it wasn't hard, within five minutes he was relaxing again and telling her a funny story about the last film he had made.

It was an hour later when Sasha caught sight of her watch and exclaimed: 'My God, look at the time—gone one o'clock!'

Jake was smoking a thin cigar with a glass of brandy in his hand. Lazily he beckoned to the head waiter. 'I'll order up a taxi, pay the bill and see you back to your flat,' he said. 'I can pick up my car later.'

As he shepherded her towards the door shortly afterwards, they passed a party of new arrivals. Sasha barely noticed them, but heard Jake exchange a few words with one. It wasn't until she was outside, climbing into the waiting taxi, that she remembered the man's face, and her heart sank. He was one of Fleet Street's most notorious gossip columnists; she could only hope that he wouldn't hear her name anywhere. Lucky that he had been with friends, he had given her a speculative look in passing, but there hadn't been time for him to start adding two and two and making an astronomical sum of it.

In the taxi she and Jake talked casually. Traffic was much lighter now and they were soon at her flat. Jake peered out at the building. 'I'd better see you to your door,' he said as she got out.

'No, it's quite okay, I'll be quite safe. Thank you for a very pleasant evening,' she said.

He got out, ignoring her gabbled phrases. Sasha said: 'Goodnight, thanks,' and hurried towards the house, afraid that he might try to kiss her if she didn't disappear rapidly.

As she unlocked the front door she heard the taxi drive away and gave a sigh of relief—which was premature, because the next second she sensed a movement and whirled round to find Jake at her side. He took the keys from her hand, pushing the door wide open.

'I think I need some black coffee before I drive myself home,' he said coolly.

Sasha began to splutter: 'Oh, no, I'm sorry, but . . . now, look . . .'

Jake was already on the stairs. She closed the front door very quietly so as not to alert Mrs Hughes who, if she was to be believed, was a victim of chronic insomnia and heard every creak of the stairs after ten p.m. Flushed and breathless, she ran after Jake, whispering agitatedly: 'Mr Redway, please—I can't make you coffee . . .'

He was outside her front door by the time she caught up with him and inserting the key into the lock. Sasha tried to wriggle past him and an undignified struggle would have taken place, all in deathly silence since she did not want to arouse her neighbours and Jake was apparently convulsed with laughter which made him incapable of speaking, if Jake had not lifted her with both hands meeting round her waist and carried her into the flat, depositing her on the nearest chair like a doll.

He shut the front door and switched on the light. Sasha blinked furiously at him. 'How dare you force your way in here! Get out before I call the police!'

He was taking off his jacket, a proceeding which alarmed her even further. 'I'll make the coffee,' he said, slinging the jacket on to a chair and walking towards the kitchenette.

Sasha sat watching him, her brain working at the speed of a comotose tortoise. She had drunk too much wine, she just wanted to go to sleep. 'I'm tired!' she wailed suddenly. 'Oh, why don't you go home? I don't want you here.' She was past being polite or making excuses, she just told him the truth. 'If you think I'm going to bed with you, think again; I'm too tired.'

Jake walked towards her; very tall and lean in his formal shirt and dark trousers, his tie off and the collar open. Sasha rose hastily, alarmed by something in his expression; the strong, sallow-skinned planes of his face locked in a tension which she glimpsed in the blue eyes, too.

'I'm a little bit tired myself,' he said grimly. 'Tired of hearing you tell me you don't want to go to bed with me—I haven't asked you yet. Maybe I should get around to it now, this obsession of yours is irritating me, perhaps if I do what you keep accusing me of intending to do it will shut you up.'

'Don't be ridiculous,' Sasha stammered, backing. There wasn't far to back, the next moment she was against the wall with nowhere to go and Jake was in front of her, his blue eyes staring down into her own.

'Is this what you want?' he whispered, his head moving slowly downwards, and she froze, dumbly staring at his mouth, hypnotised by the male curve of it as it came closer. Jake's hand moved slowly up her arm, over her bare shoulder to her throat, the skin-on-skin contact electrifying; his lips warmly touched her mouth and Sasha felt her own lips part, heard her heart begin to beat heavily as a melting heat flowed inside her, a sensual hunger waking deep in her body. Jake kissed her deeply, his fingers on her neck, stroking delicately from her ear down to the low neckline. For a moment she stood shaking while he kissed her, her arms hanging by her sides, feeling the tides of passion crashing through her, helplessly aware that she wanted him to kiss her, she needed to touch him, be close to him. That was what she had wanted in the theatre, when she stumbled and he held her briefly. A desire she had not felt for years had lit inside her, she had ached with shamed frustration. She ached with it now, her arms went up around his neck, she kissed him back, curving towards him and aware of the firm, male body pressed against her from breast to thigh.

Her eyes closed, she gave way to the feelings she hated to admit, her mind too tired to leash her clamouring body, groaning as her head fell back under the power of his kiss, her hands moving in his thick, warm hair. Jake's hand softly moved, undid her zip, she felt his cool fingers sliding down her naked back and her body arched in helpless pleasure. She touched him and felt sexual tension in him, in the strong muscles of neck and back, in the wide shoulders; the desire in her own body now so powerful that she barely knew her own identity or his, she only knew one driving impulse, a need to be so close to him that they were one flesh.

Then Jake lifted his mouth and stood looking at her and dazedly she opened her eyes, shivering with cold and the slow drain of excited feeling in her.

'Have you slept with anyone since your husband died?' he asked abruptly, his voice hoarse.

Sasha was still shuddering with the shock of her own emotions. Involuntarily she shook her head, unable to speak.

Jake was frowning darkly. 'Did you sleep with him before your marriage?'

'No, of course not,' she said, then flushed even deeper. 'My parents made me promise not to,' she said. 'We waited.' Then she shook violently, her teeth chattering. 'We waited,' she said again, and hot tears forced themselves through her lowered lids. She was shaking from head to foot, and Jake put his arms round her and pulled her back against him. This time there was no desire between them, he stroked her hair while she cried with rough, painful gulps which were wrenched deep out of her, and she didn't even think of him except as a comforting presence, she cried for Philip and herself, for the few brief days of happiness in the sun which had ended so suddenly and without warning.

She had thought she had absorbed all the pain long ago, she had believed she had cried herself out then, but now she discovered how wrong she had been; when it happened she had barely cried at all, she had been too dumb with shock, too icy with disbelief. She could remember days when she hadn't spoken, hadn't moved, had sat and stared at nothing for hours on end as if turned to stone. That was how it had felt, as if she had become a statue, not a living woman, a thing of marble without a heart. People had spoken and she had not heard them, people had moved across her vision like shadows on a blind, meaningless to her.

Gradually she had emerged from the living darkness, but by then it had been too late for tears, the pain had all been forced down inside her; a frozen block of anguish which never thawed. It had melted now, in the heat of her own desire and Jake Redway's passionate caresses: she felt it bursting up out of her, hurting her throat, hard deep cries of grief which left her raw.

She cried until there were no more tears left, then for a moment she stood in Jake's arms, weak and shivering as if with cold. Over her head he said: 'I thought you'd never stop,' and his voice was flat and remote.

'I'm sorry,' she whispered.

'Don't be stupid,' he muttered. His arms fell away from her, he stepped back. 'You'd better get some sleep, you must be exhausted.'

She nodded, head bent because she did not want him to see her red and swollen eyes, her tear-smudged face. 'Thank you, you've been very . . .'

'Go to bed,' he said harshly, and she flinched, jumping away. 'Sorry,' he said impatiently. 'I'm tired, too, this has been a difficult night for both of us.' He hesitated. 'I'd offer to sleep on the couch if I thought you wouldn't misinterpret the suggestion.'

'You should be able to get a taxi at the end of the street,' Sasha stammered.

'Will you be okay if I leave?' he asked, still hesitating.

'Fine,' she said, urgently wanting him to go, and he slowly opened the door.

'Goodnight, then.'

She murmured a reply, he looked at her, given nothing but a view of her bent black head, then went out and closed the door quietly behind him.

Sasha stood listening to his soft footsteps. She heard the outer door open and close and heard him walk away down the street. She felt drained, dead, grey. It was all she could do to go into her bedroom, undress, climb into bed and put out the light. She slept at once, barely aware of the instant when her mind loosed its hold on awareness, and if she dreamt she did not remember it in the morning.

CHAPTER SIX

SASHA caught the early train down to Millton; staring out at green fields glittering in a haze of sunlight, blue shadows among trees and the cowls of Kent oasthouses rising behind orchards heavy with ripening fruit. It was a peaceful scene. She suddenly remembered Philip talking of buying a country cottage one day, and sighed with a regret no longer bitter. What would their life together have been like? Useless to wonder that now; she was a different person. She would never know how she would have developed if she had not lost Philip. At twenty, wild and emotional and lacking self-control, she had needed Philip's inner stability, but his death had made her grow up; forced her back on her own unsuspected inner reserves. She would not now need to lean on anyone, she thought, frowning.

Caro looked surprised when she saw her. 'I thought Jake would drive you back!'

'No, I caught the train.' Was Caro disappointed? Had she been counting the hours until she saw Jake? Sasha felt an odd twinge of irritation. She turned away to kiss Madeleine, who was sitting at the kitchen table, colouring with fat bright crayons.

'We were just deciding to have a picnic,' Caroline said, sounding lighthearted now, and Sasha wondered if she had shrugged off her disappointment over Jake, or if she was acting that gay mood.

'Pic nic,' said Madeleine, making it two very excited words. 'Pic nic. Pic nic.'

'We get the point, darling,' said Caro, ruffling her curls. 'It's her new word,' she told Sasha, who laughed. 'Why don't we have coffee and you can tell me all about the Gerrard play while Mrs Carter finishes off the picnic basket. I've boiled eggs and made some rolls, there's some cold chicken and fruit and cheese.' She was leaning over a neatly packed wicker basket as she recited, checking off the items one by one. 'Do you think that will be enough?' I was expecting Jake, I thought he'd enjoy a country picnic; maybe there's too much for three. Never mind.' She straightened, smiling, but Sasha was sure there was a shadow in the slanting green eyes.

Turning to pour them both some coffee, Caro handed her a cup. 'I'm dying to hear about the first night, I read some reviews in the morning papers—it was a hit, I gather.'

'A palpable hit,' said Sasha, and Caro groaned at the quote.

They went off to drink their coffee in the sitting-room. Sasha enjoyed giving Caro a vivid account of the play, but all the time, as she talked, she was conscious of what had followed after the curtain fell for the last time, and she couldn't quite meet Caro's eyes. She felt guilty, which was ridiculous; Caro was married to another man, Jake Redway did not belong to her. Or did he? Sasha remembered seeing them standing at the window yesterday, faces in shadow. She had felt so clearly the bond between them, felt it even more deeply than she ever had watching them talking or laughing in public. It had disturbed her then, it disturbed her even more today.

'The picnic's ready and Madeleine's wanting to set off,' Mrs Carter informed them, putting her head round the door.

'We're coming,' said Caro, laughing, and got up at once. 'Naughty of Jake to let you find your own way back—I must tick him off when I see him.'

'No,' Sasha said abruptly, and Caro looked round at her, surprised by her sharp tone. 'I preferred to come by train,' Sasha explained, flushing under her stare. She did not want Caro and Jake Redway talking about her—it would be too humiliating. Would he tell Caro about how they first met? Sasha got the impression he hadn't done so yet, and he certainly wouldn't tell Caro he had kissed her like that last night.

Why had he? She had been turning that question over in her head all the way down from London. *Why* had Jake Redway kissed her? Why had he insisted on coming in to the flat? Why . . . she pushed away the urgent flood of unanswerable questions, biting her lower lip. There was an explanation, of course; not one she found very palatable. He might merely be a sexual opportunist. He might have picked up from her in the theatre that nagging physical need, her body might have communicated it to him when he touched her.

She wasn't sure why she found that idea so painful: whether because it left her feeling exposed, ashamed, grubby, or because of what it revealed about Jake Redway.

There was so much she did not know about what went on inside his head, about the truth of his private life. Was he in love with Caroline Fox? What sort of man was he behind the public glitter? Last night, over supper, she had found herself liking him very much. They had discovered a lot in common; writers, plays, people, not to mention ideas and attitudes. Such intangible things, so deceptive—ideas dissolve in the acid of the personality, what had all that he had said told her about the man behind the mask? Nothing.

She was brought back to her unanswered question: why had he started to make love to her? She had been so obsessed by her own emotions at the time that she had not had attention to spare to watch his, or work out his motives, and now in the calmer light of day she couldn't understand him at all.

It took them nearly half an hour to find a pleasant spot for the picnic. They took a narrow grassy footpath under overhanging lime trees whose branches made a semi-arch above their heads, the moving patterns of shade and light thrown ahead of them as they strolled along talking.

'How do you get on with Jake?' Caro asked, and Sasha murmured warily, 'Okay.'

'He can be bloody-minded,' Caro said. Sasha laughed without much humour.

'I'd noticed.'

They walked along the hedge of a field of barley in single file for a few moments and did not talk. The pale greeny-yellow stalks whispered and bent whiskered heads like confidential old men, a small brown bird flew up from the edge of the field, whirring, and Madeleine pointed with a plump pink finger. 'Brid.'

'Bird,' her mother corrected.

'Brid,' Madeleine insisted, twisting her bonneted head to glare at her mother. In her pretty candy-pink smocked dress and matching bonnet she looked Victorian, a primly outraged expression on her face.

'She *does* look like your husband,' Sasha said, very struck by a resemblance around the jawline, and Caro chuckled.

'Poor Madeleine! You're absolutely right, that's James when somebody argues with him, she's his image.'

'He adores her,' Sasha said, walking close to the thick hedge, the scent of grass and flowers drifting up to her as she walked. Caro was just in front of her, a summer breeze stirring the light redgold strands of hair clinging to her nape. She glanced round, an odd expression in her eyes, and Sasha looked away. She liked Caro, but this morning she felt antagonistic to her, she wasn't sure why; couldn't Caro make up her mind which of the two men she wanted? Or did she prefer to have them both dancing on her string? Was she that sort of woman, one who cannot bear to relinquish any possession even if she no longer really wants it?

They climbed over a stile, lifting Madeleine over from one to the other of them while she laughed enthusiastically, kicking her feet, then they wandered along a lush green meadow bordering a reed-lined river.

'Here, I think,' Caro decided, looking around with a hand shading her eyes. The sun dazzled along the water a hundred feet away, but along the verge of the meadow ran an irregular line of elms and oaks. Caro pushed the little girl into the shade of one of the oaks and flung herself down, sun-flushed, breathless. Sasha watched her, prickling;

Caro was slender and very alive, her eyes vivid with enjoyment, her bright hair pushed back from her neck with one hand. She made Sasha feel colourless.

'I'm so hot!' Caro looked at her, frowning. 'Sit down, Sasha, aren't you tired after that hike over the fields?'

Sasha knelt and released Madeleine from her push-chair, lifting her out. The child began to toddle about, picking buttercups. Sasha busied herself unpacking the picnic basket while Caro lay on her side and watched her daughter.

'Is anything wrong?' she asked quietly.

Sasha didn't look up. 'No, everything's here,' she said, deliberately misunderstanding her, and felt Caro watching her. 'Why don't you rest while I play with Madeleine, then we can eat later?'

Caro turned on to her back and stared up at the shifting oak branches, their fretted green leaves casting strange shadows on her face and body. 'If you ever need to talk, I'll be happy to listen and I don't repeat what I'm told,' she said.

'Nothing to tell,' Sasha said flippantly, and got up. The last person she would confide in was Caro Fox; she was too much a part of what was bothering Sasha. People were always warning you about the danger of triangles—they didn't ever say that boxes were even more dangerous. Sasha did not want to form the fourth side of a box which enclosed such explosive emotions. It was enough of a problem merely being an observer, she had no intention of becoming part of that situation.

Catching up with Madeleine as she headed for the delightful and potentially dangerous river bank, she took the child's wriggling hand and led her, safely tethered, to the edge to stare down into the slowly moving, reedy, weedy water.

'Fiss,' said Madeleine, enchanted.

They both gazed down and saw a minute brown speckled shape under a green mass of weed.

'I think it *was* a fish,' Sasha said, surprised.

'Fiss,' Madeleine repeated, satisfied. She liked to have her speculations about the world confirmed. She was a child with a very high opinion of her own intelligence and rather a low one of that of the adults around her; but she was a conformist, she worked inside the system, she knew who got her brown egg for tea and her bowl of cornflakes for breakfast.

Sasha walked along the bank, holding Madeleine's hand tightly, and looked back to see from Caro's relaxed limbs and closed eyes that she had drifted into a light sleep. 'Shall we paddle for a while?' she asked Madeleine, who nodded eagerly. They removed Madeleine's white socks and shoes and Sasha slid out of her sandals to step down gingerly into the cool water.

Madeleine splashed a foot, laughing. 'Not too vigorously,' Sasha begged, moving a little away while still clutching the small hand. Flies buzzed and danced under the trees, the air was heavy with heat and fragrant with the scent of grass and flowers. Sasha should have been happy, it was a marvellous day, yet she felt impatience and restless urgency drumming in her veins. Something was lacking, she wasn't sure what; only that she missed something that she felt should be a vital ingredient of the summer day.

They waded back to the bank, water swirling around their ankles. Sasha dried Madeleine's feet lightly with a handkerchief, watching the sluggish river move around tall bulrushes whose reflections moved, shimmering, on the surface. As she stood up, Sasha leaned over and saw her own face, fragmented on the rippling water, and knew why she felt that restless ache. She wanted someone there to share that lovely day with her, someone who belonged to her the way Philip had, someone special to have secrets, jokes with; rush to with news, relax with when she was tired, someone to belong to and care about.

Madeleine landed on her sleeping mother who gasped and jack-knifed up, laughing. 'Fiss,' Madeleine told her, pointing. 'Watter.'

Caro kissed her and Sasha envied them; she looked at Caro with impatient dismay. Caroline Fox had a husband who loved her and an adorable little girl—what did she think she was doing, risking all that by having a secret affair with another man?

That evening James Fox arrived just in time for dinner, stripping off his tie as he walked into the sitting-room, his face tired. He flung his briefcase and an evening newspaper on to a chair and kissed Caro, who had raised a sun-flushed face to him, smiling. 'Have a good day, darling?'

'Exhausting,' he said. 'But satisfactory. Madeleine asleep?'

'Ages ago, she was yawning by five o'clock. We had a picnic by the river and she tired herself out running after a ball.'

'I hope you kept a watchful eye on her, if you were down by the river,' he said, his thin brows frowning, and Caro eyed him with impatient amusement.

'Of course! Don't fuss, James!'

'She takes after you, far too reckless. I don't want her falling into that water.'

'Sasha wouldn't let that happen,' Caro said wryly. 'Would you, Sasha? She didn't leave Madeleine alone for a second.'

James Fox turned and surveyed Sasha thoughtfully, one brow lifting. She was sitting cross-legged in a chair, and felt uneasy under that cool stare, but then James always made her feel like that, he was a disturbing man, those keen eyes far too piercing, horribly intelligent. They made her feel very young and transparent. She would not like to face him in a cross-examination even if she had nothing to hide; if she was concealing anything she felt he would prise it out of her in double quick time.

'Have you seen an evening paper?' he asked, startling her.

'No,' she stammered, and he bent to pick up the one he had brought in with him.

'You've made the gossip column in this one,' he told her.

'What?' Caro asked, laughing. 'Really? Let me see ...'

James opened the newspaper, flicked over the pages and handed it to Caroline open around the centre.

'What does it say?' Sasha was hot and worried; she guessed that the item was about Jake Redway, what else could it be? She had felt uneasy when she saw that gossip columnist at the Café Royal, he had given her an odd smile. Had he attended the first night, too? Had he seen her with Jake there? Or had he gone on to the first night party and picked up gossip about her and Jake from someone who had been in Peter's dressing-room?

Caroline was reading, her red-gold head bent so that Sasha could not see her face. She looked up slowly, her expression unreadable, and handed Sasha the paper without saying a word. Sasha hurriedly read the little item, her face burning as she took in what it said.

'Guess what lucky little actress is being seen around with Jake Redway these days?' it said coyly, and went on to describe Sasha as a sexy brunette with an eye on the top. 'And Jake is the man to help her get there,' the columnist ended.

'How can they print stuff like that?' Sasha burst out angrily, looking up. 'It makes me sound like a scheming, unscrupulous little bitch! He's implying that I'm dating Jake for what I can get out of it!'

'Don't worry about it, nobody who knows you is going to take any notice of that sort of innuendo,' said James with calm indifference, and she flung the newspaper away, barely coherent with rage.

'Some people may, they do believe what they read in newspapers. Jake may; he might think I'm trying to use him for my career—it isn't true, but I can hardly go about with a placard denying it. What a rotten thing to say! What sort of person thinks like that?'

'Someone with a cynical, hard-boiled attitude.' James stood watching her, his hands in his pockets, his eyes wry. 'To be fair to the man, he's probably seen a lot of women on the make, the world is full of them. Jake Redway is a man with influence and money, and men like that have no difficulty attracting pretty girls, but I'm certain your friends aren't going to believe a word of this smear story. Forget it, everyone else will very soon.'

'Including Jake?' Sasha muttered, still ·very flushed.

'Jake's far too experienced to be taken in by gossip stories. You can be sure he's often come up against the sort of journalist who writes them, and Jake's too shrewd to believe you're the sort of calculating little career-climber this man is hinting at—Jake will ignore the story. You should do the same.'

Out of the corner of her eye, Sasha saw Caroline's blank face. She hadn't said a syllable, she hadn't given a flicker of reaction—what was she thinking? What had she thought as she read the item?

It was only later, when she was in bed and unable to sleep, that she recalled saying: 'He's implying that I'm dating Jake for what I can get out of it.' What had Caroline made of that? Sasha had not realised at the time that her own words made it sound as though she and Jake were lovers, her angry response must have underlined what the gossip columnist had said. She hadn't picked her words carefully, she had blurted out the first ones which came into her head, and only afterwards did it dawn on her what she had said.

Next day Caroline did not get up, and when Sasha went downstairs to breakfast Mrs Carter told her that Caroline had a summer cold. 'Sneezing her head off, she is—her throat sounds like a foghorn, too. Stay in bed, I told her. She can be pigheaded sometimes, but she saw the sense of that. Best place for her with a cold.'

Sasha took up a glass of warm milk at ten-thirty and Caroline lifted a heavy head, smiling gloomily.

'Sorry to land you with Madeleine.'

'Don't be silly, that's what I'm here for—she's no trouble. You stay there and rest.' Looking at Caroline's flushed face and shadowed eyes, Sasha felt guilty. She hadn't slept very well herself, and she had been feeling very antagonistic to Caro as she lay awake and thought about Jake Redway and James and Madeleine. Caroline had so much, why was she hanging on to Jake? If he was in love with her it would be kinder to cut him free than to cling on when she was not prepared to give up her husband and child for him.

Sasha went back downstairs and took Madeleine for a walk to the village to buy groceries Mrs Carter said were needed. They wandered along in a leisurely way and looked at shop windows, then walked back, staying in the shade of the hedge. The sun was very hot, the air still. Sasha saw wild strawberries growing deep among the green leaves and grass at the foot of the hedge; she picked a few and shared them with Madeleine. Sweet and cool, they were tiny but delicious, slipping down the throat before you had done more than taste them.

After a light lunch, Madeleine took her usual nap, and Sasha went out into the garden in a blue bikini to sun herself; she had acquired a smooth golden tan during the past two weeks. It suited her skin and colouring, gave her dark blue eyes more depth and brilliance and made her curly black hair seem more dramatic. She lay on her tummy and undid her bikini top so that the sun could tan her back more evenly. Eyes half-closed, she watched an ant staggering along between blades of grass, carrying a piece of leaf. Suddenly a foot appeared, the ant hurried out of sight, and Sasha's drowsy mood evaporated and she glanced up the lean length of Jake Redway's body to the amused face bent to watch her.

'Oh, it's you,' she said, starting to sit up, only to realise that she could hardly do that while her top was undone. Very pink, she fumbled with the clasp of the cotton strap and Jake knelt down.

'Let me,' he said in a tone threaded with mockery.

She was in no position to argue. His long, cool fingers brushed her bare back as he clipped the strap in place and she felt a shiver run down her spine.

'You look very sexy in that,' he drawled as she sat up. 'How long have you been out here?'

'Half an hour or so—Caroline's in bed with a bad cold and Madeleine's asleep,' she stammered, still off balance at the shock of seeing him.

'So Mrs Carter told me,' he nodded. 'You look very hot, you don't want to get sunstroke.' He ran a finger smoothly down her naked arm and a tremor of reaction shot through her; she looked down, her mouth dry. She felt as though she wasn't wearing anything at all; Jake's eyes were moving over her, narrowed and assessing, missing out nothing in that leisurely inspection, making her intensely aware of her own body and his powerful masculinity. He leaned over and picked up the bottle of suntan lotion, unscrewed it and tipped it over his palm. 'You need some more of this,' he told her, and she stiffened.

'I put some on before I started sunbathing.' She did not want him to touch her again, she didn't know if she could stand it, the intimacy of his skin against her own made her body ache in a way she hated.

'Your skin's burning,' he observed, staring at her, and how could she tell him that if she was flushed it was because of him, not because the sun was so hot? 'Sit still,' he ordered, and the next moment she felt the cool cream touch her heated skin as Jake began to smooth the lotion into her shoulders, pushing aside the thin straps, his fingertips softly sliding from the base of her pulsing throat to her rounded shoulderbone. Sasha did not dare to move; she sat, head lowered, watching him through her lashes, terrified that he would notice and guess at the reason for the uneven roughness of her breathing.

He was wearing a thin white shirt, open at the collar, and white pants pulled in tightly at his slim waist, his body visibly lithe and muscled under the tightly fitting clothes. Sasha couldn't take her eyes off him. He seemed too preoccupied with smoothing the lotion into her skin to be aware of her gaze; she could look at him without being in any danger of meeting his eyes. His lids were half lowered over those bright blue eyes, his smoky lashes flickering as he concentrated on his task, his firm mouth slightly parted as he breathed, the curving line of it suggesting a sexual power which the rest of his body asserted with even more explosive force. She stared at the graining of his skin; each tiny pore and line clearly visible to her at such close quarters. Every time he breathed she felt her heart constrict.

She was angry with herself, she grew even more heated, but she couldn't tear her eyes away from him. She ached to touch him, she wanted him to go on touching her. It was a physical hunger she couldn't control, it had nothing to do with emotion; she was not in love with him, she told herself, she was not even sure she liked him. She didn't approve of his pursuit of Caro Fox; didn't he ever consider what he was doing to Caro's family? Sasha told herself she despised him, she had nothing but contempt for him, yet inside her she felt that painful, nagging need to feel that hard mouth moving against her own, the way it had the other night.

His hands had moved down the wide length of her arms, but when he picked up the bottle of lotion again she sat back on her heels, shaking her head. 'That's enough,' she said sharply. 'I'm going in now, anyway.' She did not want him to go any further with that intimate, disturbing little massage, it was doing drastic things to her heartbeat.

He looked up, mouth ironic. 'Sure?' he asked mockingly, and Sasha suddenly wondered if he had been so unaware of her stare, after all. There was a dangerous gleam in the blue eyes, and she did not like his smile, it held far too much self-confidence.

She stood up and Jake rose, too, handing her the bottle of lotion and the book she had left on the grass.

'Did you read the evening paper yesterday?' he asked as they walked towards the house, and Sasha stopped in her tracks, turning a distressed face towards him.

'Yes, I was appalled.'

He shrugged. 'Don't upset yourself over that gutter innuendo, the man always works like that. Have you had any follow-up attempts yet?'

'No, thank heavens,' said Sasha with a sigh of relief.

Jake glanced at her sideways, his mouth crooked. 'You will. I've had calls all day—that's why I came down here to see you. They won't know where to find you until somebody lets the cat out of the bag. Do any of your friends know you're staying here?'

'I don't know—Maggie, of course, but she wouldn't tell anyone.'

'Unless she already has! Once she knows the press are on your tail, she'll clam up, but God knows how many people she's already told that you're working for Caro.' He stopped talking and looked up the stairs as they walked across the hall. Sasha glanced up, too, and saw Caroline smile down at him; a vivid, impulsive smile which lit her whole face. Sasha's throat closed up and she swallowed painfully.

'I thought I heard your voice,' said Caroline, leaning on the banister. 'I won't come down, I've got a ghastly cold and I don't want to give it to you.' She was wearing a low-necked white silk nightdress and over that a matching negligee foaming with delicately patterned white lace. Her skin was pale, her eyes shadowed, her red-gold hair tousled, but she looked lovely, and Sasha looked away, torn between a grey misery and anger.

'How are you?' Jake asked with loving gentleness, and Sasha hated him, too. He had no business talking to another man's wife with such feeling in his voice.

'I feel as though my head was full of cottonwool,' Caroline laughed.

'Go back to bed, darling,' Jake said. 'You shouldn't be wandering about while you're ill. You don't take enough care of yourself.'

Caroline put her fingers to her lips and blew him a teasing kiss. 'Bully!' She glanced at Sasha's stiff face. 'Madeleine's awake, could you come and get her, Sasha?'

'Of course,' Sasha said politely.

'See you, Jake darling,' said Caroline, vanishing, and Sasha went upstairs and picked up Madeleine. The little girl was warm and soft, face flushed from sleep, eyes bright and lively. Sasha kissed her and Madeleine put her arms around her neck, half strangling her in a passionate hug.

Sasha carried her to the bathroom and washed her face and hands, then took her to her mother's room to say hello. Madeleine wriggled, trying to get down, and Caroline said: 'No, darling, I can't kiss you—you might catch my cold. Go down and have some nice lemonade, Mrs Carter just made some for me.' She had a glass of fresh lemonade in her hand, sipping it from time to time. Her voice was low and husky, her throat was still sore. She smiled at Sasha, 'Sorry to land you with her all day, like this. Summer colds don't last long, I should be better tomorrow.'

'It doesn't matter, she's no trouble at all,' said Sasha, wishing she did not like Caroline so much.

'James rang to say he's coming home early, so you and Jake could go out once he's back.'

Sasha flushed, and took Madeleine away without answering. Was Caroline discreetly suggesting she remove Jake from James Fox's vicinity? Whenever Sasha saw the two men together she felt tension buzzing in the air; James Fox was always coldly polite, Jake was blandly mocking in return; so far they had not come to open hostilities, but Sasha always felt they might.

How could Caroline allow this situation to go on? Did she get fun out of seeing the two men snarling at each other over her? Would she prolong their jealousy and rivalry for ever simply because she did not want to choose finally between them? Didn't she want to choose?

So many questions, no answers, and Sasha couldn't ask Caroline for the truth; even if Caroline knew it, she wouldn't be likely to tell it. If Caroline did get a kick out of having the two men fighting for her, she was not going to admit it.

When Madeleine saw Jake she held her arms out to him and he sat down with her on his lap, talking to her while Sasha fetched a glass of home-made lemonade and a biscuit for her.

When Sasha returned to the sitting-room she found Jake and Madeleine building a house with a large box of coloured wooden bricks. Madeleine sat on Jake's lap while she drank her lemonade and nibbled her biscuit, talking to him trustingly, her head on his arm. Sasha looked at his strong profile angrily—how could he smile at the child like that, when he would wreck her family life if he could?

Jake laughed at something Madeleine said, glanced round and caught that expression on Sasha's face. He frowned, his black brows shooting up, his blue eyes losing their smile and becoming narrowed and hard. Sasha looked away, but felt him watching her for a moment until Madeleine chattered on again and Jake's attention was focused on her for a while.

Half an hour later the house had become a small palace; Jake improvised with empty cotton reels for stools and matchboxes for beds and cupboards, and Madeleine excitedly brought small toys to put inside the tiny rooms.

'You look busy,' a cool voice said from the door, and Madeleine jumped up to hold her arms out to her father.

James strolled forward to pick her up, his dry gaze on Jake's face as he lifted his daughter. 'Hallo, Redway, here again?' The question was lightly delivered but held a cutting edge.

'I can't keep away,' Jake retorted just as coolly.

'I've noticed,' James murmured, kissing his daughter. 'How's Caroline?' he asked Sasha over Madeleine's head.

'She looks pale,' Jake answered for her, and James slowly turned his head to look at him, his eyebrows level.

'She's up?'

'No,' said Jake, smiling, and Sasha felt her nerves burn with angry fire. Under the calm exchange there was that incessant needling of each other which she found so disturbing.

Hurriedly she said: 'Mrs Fox said hello from the top of the stairs, she didn't come down because she doesn't want anyone to catch her cold.'

Jake smiled at James Fox, who regarded him drily. 'I'll go up and see her,' James said. 'Now that I'm home you're free to go out if you like, Sasha. I'll keep an eye on Madeleine.' He went out, carrying the little girl, and Jake raised one eyebrow.

'Why don't we have a drive and find a nice country pub to eat at? I know several which do a terrific dinner.'

'No, thank you,' Sasha said icily. 'I suggest you

drive back to London. Mrs Fox won't get up, and nobody else wants you here.' The words came out like knives.

There was a silence. Jake stared at her, slowly going red.

CHAPTER SEVEN

'THAT wasn't the impression I got when we were out in the garden earlier,' Jake said fiercely, taking an aggressive step towards her. Sasha backed, her teeth fastening into the soft inner skin of her lips and her skin beginning to burn with humiliation. He had picked up what she was feeling, after all; she had been afraid he might, and she wished she could run away from those angrily mocking blue eyes, but she didn't; she faced him, her expression defiant.

'I don't know what you're talking about,' she lied, and he laughed shortly.

'Of course you do, my instincts work pretty well, I could feel it—you may hate feeling like that, but you're only lying to yourself if you pretend you're indifferent to me.'

Sasha swallowed on a bitter taste, feeling sick, but she nerved herself to answer him. 'I'm not indifferent to you, I despise you!' Her tone was loaded with contempt and Jake's face darkened, his eyes watching her intently as she stared back at him.

'Despite me?' he repeated. 'For God's sake, Sasha, you can't go on blaming me for something that isn't my fault—it isn't rational; it isn't bloody fair. I won't be made the scapegoat for what happened!'

For a moment she was too confused to answer, and her lips parted on a puzzled gasp. She had forgotten Philip for a little while, she had been so caught up in angry reaction to the triangle in this house. Jake watched her shifting expressions.

'You've got to get it into perspective,' he said in a slightly calmer voice. 'You had a rough deal losing your husband on your honeymoon, of course you were distraught at the time and I was around, so all your anger was focused on me, I understand that, but that all happened three years ago. Three years, for God's sake! How much longer are you going to brood over it?'

'I'm not . . .' she began, and he broke in on her stammered words vehemently:

'Oh, yes, so you imagine I don't know what you're thinking when you stare at me like that? I look round and your face is full of hostility . . . I'm tired of it!' He took another step and his fingers gripped her arms so tightly she felt the pressure of his nails in her flesh. He shook her, his face bent towards her, only inches away. 'Do you hear me, Sasha? I'm sick of being blamed for something which wasn't my fault!'

'I wasn't talking about that,' she stammered, trying to pull away and helpless in the vice of his grip. 'And I don't want to talk about it, either.'

'I'm sure you don't,' Jake muttered, staring at her mouth, his lids half down over his eyes and a strange, intent look on his face. Sasha's mouth went dry, she began to tremble, aware of a new tension in the air. 'You don't want to face what you're feeling because it scares you,' he said huskily. 'I'm willing to bet you haven't let yourself look at another man since he died, you've walled yourself up in the past because you feel so bitter. You've given it away every time we've talked about him. Your parents made you wait two years; when you're in love two years is a whole lifetime, and then just as you finally came together he died . . . you've been as frustrated as hell ever since, but because of the way it happened you're angry, too, aren't you? Angry and scared—you can't risk feeling anything for anyone else because you loved him and lost him, you're resentful because of all that bottled up need. You're a lady with a lot of mental problems, Sasha, and I am fed up to the back teeth with being treated as if it was all my fault.'

'At least I didn't create my problems,' Sasha threw back angrily. 'Mine just happened to me— you're busy creating problems for yourself, Mr Redway. Which of us needs a psychiatrist, you or me?'

'What the hell are you gibbering about now?' he asked, frowning blackly.

'Mrs Fox,' Sasha said and his eyes hardened, his expression stiffening.

'Caro? What about her?'

'You know exactly what I mean!' She gave him a distasteful smile, her chin lifted.

He held her at arms' length, staring at her; his face concentrated, tense, the strong mouth level and hard, the blue eyes probing her flushed face as he tried to work out what she meant. Sasha's eyes threw contemptuous defiance at him despite the fact that she was still trembling. She was not going to let him see how deeply he affected her. He had just told her she was frustrated, she knew all about that, but she didn't see why Jake Redway should feel he had any right to discuss her private problems, any more than she could bear to admit to him that she was having to fight a wild sexual attraction every time he came near her.

'You don't know what you're talking about,' Jake said at last, flatly.

'Don't I? I've been living in this house for several weeks now— do you think I could fail to notice that Mr Fox can't stand the sight of you, or that you take every opportunity you get to come down here?'

His fingers tightened, and she winced. 'You're hurting!'

'Good,' he muttered. 'You deserve it. You think I'm having an affair with Caro, is that it?'

She hesitated, reluctant to answer because it was painful to put her suspicions into words. Although it was such a warm day she felt cold in the thin cotton tunic she had slipped over her bikini when she first came back into the house from the sunny garden; the back of her neck had gone icy cold, her flush had died. She felt a wild misery sweep through her and Jake waited, watching her intently.

'Well, go on,' he muttered harshly. 'Don't go dumb on me now.' He moved closer, threat in every powerful line of his long body; she saw the muscles in his brown throat move convulsively as he swallowed, and the white shirt rose and fell rapidly as he breathed. 'I want to know—do you think I'm having an affair with Caro?'

'Yes, I'd be interested to know that, too,' said an icy voice from the door, and Jake released her, spinning round. Sasha's heart lurched, she looked across the room at James Fox and could have sunk through the floor. He was leaning in the doorway, apparently relaxed, but with a face which was rigid with control, and his eyes were deadly.

Sasha felt scalding colour rush up to her hairline. James Fox stared at her. 'Well, Sasha? You haven't answered yet. What makes you think my wife is having an affair with him?'

Her voice wouldn't come for an instant, then she stammered rustily: 'Nothing, I didn't say ... I'm sorry if ... I'm sure she isn't.'

'So am I,' said James Fox with that glacial control. 'If I wasn't certain of it I'd probably kill him.' He spoke with such a matter-of-fact decision that for a second or two she did not take in what he had actually said, and then she felt her knees give under her; she did not doubt that James Fox meant what he had said, he was not making idle threats, he was speaking calmly and without emphasis, merely stating a fact. That was what she found so terrifying. He was an alarming man.

His cold eyes moved on to Jake and Sasha looked at Jake, too. He was smiling crookedly.

'You really hate my guts, don't you?'

'Very graphically put,' James Fox said without denying it.

'You've never had any reason to worry about me,' Jake told him drily.

Equally dry, James Fox said: 'Fortunately for you. All the same, I'd be happier if I saw less of you around my home.'

'You flatter me!'

'Not intentionally.'

'I'm sure,' Jake said, smiling.

Sasha was trying to follow the conversation, a curious painful relief inside her as she realised that there was really no question of Caroline leaving her husband for Jake. Neither Jake or James Fox seemed in any doubt about that, but that did not lessen the prickly hostility between the two men. Their eyes had the guarded wariness of duellists as they talked, and Sasha's relief seeped out of her as she considered them. Jake might not hope to persuade Caroline to go away with him, but Sasha picked up very strongly the silent admission that Jake was in love with Caroline. James Fox was aware of it, every word he had said underlined his awareness and his resulting antagonism.

'Caro is trying to get some sleep, I'd rather you didn't disturb her by yelling at each other any longer,' James drawled, glancing in Sasha's direction. 'If you must quarrel, could you do it elsewhere?' He turned on his heel and vanished, and Jake slowly looked round at Sasha, who couldn't meet his eyes.

'Pleased with yourself?' he asked tersely.

She lifted her head, uneasiness in her face. 'I didn't mean him to hear, it was you who started shouting, not me.'

'That's your first reaction, isn't it? To blame somebody else for whatever happens.' Jake took hold of her elbow and hustled her towards the door. 'Come on, we're going somewhere quiet. I want to talk to you and this time you're going to listen without interruption.'

'I've listened to you for long enough!' She tugged at her imprisoned arm and Jake drew a sharp, angry breath.

'Sasha, I'm trying to be patient with you—don't provoke me or I won't be responsible for the consequences.' He pushed her across the hall and out of the front door. Sasha did not want any more trouble within earshot of James Fox, she had to let Jake put her into his car and slam the door on her. The car started with a roar of acceleration and shot away towards the gate. Jake drove in frowning silence. She risked a quick look at him through her lashes and his profile had a dark force which alarmed her; his eyes staring straight ahead, lids lowered, his mouth straight and fierce, his jaw tautly controlled. The wind blew in through the open windows and his black hair lifted with it, flying across his temples. He pushed it back with one impatient hand and looked round at her.

'You're right about one thing,' he said. 'Caro means a lot to me, she always has; I got into the habit of caring about her too long ago to stop now. The way I feel about her is all bound up with the way I feel about my job, about myself; I don't know what to call it, it's love and it isn't, not in the sense most people use the word. I care about Maggie, too, although not quite so much. Loving isn't something you can compartmentalise; it's part of living. What sort of world would this be if people couldn't care about each other without expecting to get something out of it?'

He stopped talking, and Sasha looked down, an angry compassion for him mixed up with a twisted self-pity. Jake was living with an impossible dream; she knew how it felt to live just out of reach of happiness for years. While she waited to marry Philip she had been obsessed with a nagging frustration of the senses, only to lose him and be left with a deep ache of need which would never be satisfied. It would kill her to go through such emotions again; she was afraid of being hurt again as Jake was obviously being hurt. But she had had a right to love Philip—Jake was not merely getting hurt himself, he was hurting others, and that made Sasha angry.

'Why don't you just go away and forget her? Can't you see you're just prolonging the agony?' she asked, and Jake shifted angrily, looking at her, frowning.

'We're still talking at cross purposes! Look, being in love is greedy; it wants a return, it demands a response. It's a violent emotion; as basic as hunger—and once it's satisfied it changes to something else. When you're starving you'll kill for food, but once you've sated that need you'll eat for pleasure, but you won't be prepared to commit murder to get what you want.' He sighed. 'I wouldn't kill to get Caro. I'm not in love with her. Oh, I thought I was, once, for a little while—but I was fooling myself. I still care about her. She's almost a part of myself after all these years. I'd miss her like hell if I didn't see her, it would be like losing an arm or a leg, but my whole life wouldn't fall apart.'

'Mine did when Philip died,' Sasha said in a husky voice, her eyes widening with a sense of shock as she heard the past tense in her own tone. Her life had *not* fallen apart, she realised, it had merely stopped; on that emotional level. She had refused to feel any more—she had gone on refusing until Jake forced her to look back at what she had been trying to forget; and in making her admit and remember her own pain had shown her that under the scar she had been hiding for so long a new skin, a new life, had been imperceptibly forming.

Jake sat waiting for her to say something else,

but she hurriedly looked away, and after a moment he said: 'Fox, now, he'd go to pieces if he lost her. The man's obsessed with Caro—that's why she chose him, I suppose, she knew he really loved her.' He laughed shortly. 'Women usually have a stronger intuition about these things.'

'Do they? Obviously I'm the exception that proves the rule,' Sasha muttered. 'I've made a fool of myself. Mrs Fox isn't going to like me very much after this—I only hope I haven't caused too much trouble for her.'

'Oh, Fox didn't hear anything from you that he didn't already know about,' Jake shrugged. 'It was my fault—I can never resist baiting him. It gives me a kick. He's a possessive bastard, he never has liked either me or Maggie, but he's had to learn to live with the fact that Caro likes having us around.'

'That was what made me suspect you were having an affair with her! Whenever you were there, the atmosphere was so tense!'

Jake's mouth indented. 'Okay, for Caro's sake I should quit pulling Fox's tail, I'll admit that.' He pulled over to the side of the road and pulled up, turning to look at her. 'I've been very frank with you, Sasha, are you going to return the compliment?'

She stiffened, eyes guarded. Through the open window of the car she smelt summer grass and the fugitive fragrance of wild flowers; she heard the drowsy summer sounds of the countryside, birdsong, the drone of a dark brown bumble-bee reeling from one patch of pink clover to another, drunken and replete. Jake breathed beside her and she could not look at him because her senses were fiercely alive to him in a way which terrified her. It was the first time since Philip's death that any other man had been able to crash through the barriers she had put up around herself, and she was not ready to face up to how she felt. What else had she learnt from life but that loving meant leaving yourself open to unbearable pain?

'Isn't it time you faced up to a few facts yourself?' Jake prompted, and his voice sounded closer, she looked round in shock and found him dangerously near, his eyes only inches away from her.

'Like what?' she muttered, a pulse beating fiercely in her throat. Jake stared at it and she moistened her dry lips, trembling.

'Like the fact that you're human and you need more than just a memory to live with,' he said very softly. His hand moved and she tensed; it touched her neck so lightly she shuddered at the cool brush of fingertips drifting down the curve of her throat to where that agitated little flicker betrayed her. 'Don't you?' he murmured, the tips of his fingers resting on it as though to count the rapid beat of her heart.

'I know I'm human,' she said huskily, moving to dislodge his hand without a struggle. It worked, his hand dropped away, but instead of putting it back on the wheel he let it slide down to touch her breast, and Sasha's breathing seemed to stop altogether for an instant. She went rigid, her blue eyes wide and shaken, and Jake gave her a mocking smile a second before he moved closer. She had no time to think, to decide on a reaction, the next moment his mouth was moving against her lips with a heated, languorous sensuality which made her head spin. Jake used no force, he took his time, his hand now burrowing into her ruffled black curls, shaping her parted lips underneath his own, the warm moistness of his mouth flicking the inner skin and sending a feverish wave of response through her. She felt his fingertips exploring her body with a delicacy which matched that kiss: softly stroking a path from breast to thigh, travelling down her spine, caressing her throat, the teasing movements making her weak with pleasure.

Jake raised his head a moment later and looked at her through his lashes, those blue eyes hectic with excitement. 'You see,' he murmured huskily. 'We all have to face facts sooner or later, we can't keep hankering for what we can't have, we have to settle for what we can get.'

Sasha felt coldness seeping into her. 'Take second-best, you mean,' she said, watching his face and aware of a deep, painful ache inside her body.

His eyes flickered, his mouth twisted slightly. 'Put it any way you like so long as you realise that dreaming about a dead man will only drive you nuts in the end. It's a very cold and lonely business, wanting someone you can never have— it's time you came back to life, Sasha.' His hand moved as he spoke, she felt it brush her bare thigh, and stiffened. Jake looked into her eyes as he touched her intimately and she craved the fulfilment he was offering her; she heard his breathing quicken as he restlessly moved even closer, his face flushed and tense.

'You need it,' he whispered, kissing her throat. 'We both do.' His voice deepened, rough and uneven. 'I want you, Sasha.'

She ached with desire, wanted him with an urgency which frightened her, but something held her back from the edge of total abandonment. She remembered what he had said about his feelings for Caroline Fox; that he wouldn't kill to get her. Jake's emotions were not deep enough for such all-consuming love; he had consoled himself with other women, shrugging his shoulders, and that, no doubt, was why Caroline had chosen James Fox. She had known Jake too well, she had realised how little importance he placed on love.

'You want me, too, don't you?' Jake asked huskily. 'Do you, Sasha?' He was half uncertain, half sure of himself; she caught the echo of uncertainty in his voice and her own doubts clarified.

She pushed him away. 'It isn't enough for me! I'm sure sex with you would be terrific, but it wouldn't mean a thing, would it?' She was talking in a quiet, flat voice; she had to speak like that to retain control of herself. She was facing how she really felt about him and bitterly angry with both herself and Jake.

'It's what you need! You're only half alive like this; you're living like a nun and you're a warm-blooded woman who needs . . .'

'Not just sex!' Sasha interrupted, her voice rising with anger. 'I'm not an animal; if I need a stud I can always hire one!'

Jake looked stunned, taken aback. If she hadn't been so angry she could have laughed at his expression. She wished she could hate him—he had ruthlessly forced her to emerge from the safe, emotional isolation of her grief for Philip but he should have left her locked in the glass casket of her past. He had shattered the glass without caring what would happen to her afterwards and she was exposed to real life again. She was awake and alive and vulnerable, and she was terrified that she might be falling in love with Jake Redway. What frightened her most was that she might be tempted to take the physical pleasure he was offering her now, and then she would be trapped and the only way out would be through a pain more intolerable than anything she had yet suffered, because Jake did not love her and she needed to be loved.

'Are you pretending you don't want me?' Jake asked fiercely. 'I don't believe you—if there's one subject I'm an expert on, it's love.'

'Love?' Sasha almost shouted the word. 'You don't even know what it means! You aren't capable of loving anyone but yourself—you're too selfish. You backed off from loving Caro and you know why—you could never have given her enough of yourself, your ego wouldn't let you. You're so blind, you think love is pleasure, and it isn't; it's often pain. But your instincts work okay, don't they? You refuse to love anyone enough to run the risk of getting hurt.' Her voice was bitter, she knew what she was talking about. She had not wanted to run that risk herself; Jake had forced her to leave her safe haven and now she was dangerously close to loving him.

Jake was staring at her, his lips parted, breathing audibly. Sasha swallowed and went on: 'That's why you're such a good actor, I suppose; you give everything to your work. It pays off as far as your career goes, but it makes you a bad risk for a woman.'

'Finished?' Jake snarled when she paused again.

'Not quite,' she said. 'You told me I was frustrated . . .'

'So you are,' he bit out. 'As frustrated as hell!'

'I'd be a damned sight more frustrated if I let myself get involved with you!' Sasha flared back, and then hoped she had not betrayed too much with that angry retort. But Jake gave her merely a look of stunned disbelief, offence in every line of him.

'What's that supposed to mean? You haven't given me a chance to prove you wrong,' he said savagely. 'I've never had any complaints about my performances, I can assure you.' He had totally misinterpreted what she said—but then what else had she expected? His ego was obsessed with his sexual virility, he had not understood that she was talking about feelings. Sasha gave a dry little sigh, her dormant sense of humour awakening.

'I'm sure you're technically dazzling,' she murmured, and Jake stared at her with angry blue eyes. 'It would be the lack of feeling I'd miss, though—I'd have thought an actor of your experience would have learnt by now that technique without feeling is too unsatisfactory. I might just as well sleep with a robot.'

'You little bitch!' Jake said hoarsely, darkly flushed with temper and insulted pride. He moved abruptly and Sasha jumped away from him, thinking for a second that he was going to hit her, the blinding rage in his face was murderous. But he was only starting the car; the acceleration roared and she was almost flung out of her seat as Jake put his foot down on the pedal and sent the car swerving into the road and away at a speed which was soon close to ninety miles an hour.

Before she knew it, they were back at the Fox home. Jake pulled up outside it with a grinding of brakes. He didn't look round at her and after a pause Sasha got out. The car had flashed out of the gates a moment later.

She walked into the house to find Mrs Carter in the hall, her face excited. 'Someone waiting for you, miss,' she hissed, looking over her shoulder towards the sitting room. 'A reporter!'

Sasha's heart sank, she was in no mood to talk to reporters and she could imagine what he wanted to talk about—Jake Redway, the subject Sasha least wanted to discuss with anyone.

'All right,' she said on a reluctant sigh, and went into the room to find a sharp-featured young man apparently pricing the porcelain figures on Caroline Fox's elegant bureau. He swung round and Sasha gave him a polite smile, her eyes wary.

For the next half an hour she fenced guardedly with him, denying the rumours about her and Jake and trying to talk instead about her own career. The reporter kept going back to the only subject he was interested in—Sasha kept her temper only with an effort. She was deeply relieved when he left, but she had a gloomy suspicion that all her denials would be ignored, particularly as the reporter said as he was going out: 'That was Jake Redway you were out with, wasn't it?' He grinned at her expression and went. Mrs Carter must have told him, she realised, or had he merely guessed?

Mrs Carter put her head round the door and Sasha looked at her with grim impatience. 'Mrs Fox wants a word,' Mrs Carter said.

Sasha bit her lip. 'Very well,' she said.

No prizes for guessing what Caroline Fox

wanted to say to her. She was going to be fired, and she couldn't blame Caroline for doing it, she had brought it on herself.

She found Caroline sitting up in bed in a pretty green bedjacket, fluffy angora with a wide satin frill around the neck which tied at the throat and fell in a trail of green satin ribbons. Caro was brushing her hair, it shone like polished gold as she looked across the room at Sasha's nervous face.

For a few seconds Caroline studied her in silence. Sasha waited, her hands curling at her sides. Well, get on with it, she thought miserably, tell me to pack and get the hell out of here.

Then Caro smiled suddenly, her green eyes full of teasing amusement. 'You idiot!' she said, patting the bed. 'Come and sit down and tell me what on earth is going on between you and Jake!'

Sasha sagged with relief and gratitude. She had been dreading the row she had expected, after her exchange with Jake she didn't know how she was going to go through another difficult scene. She began to walk over to the bed, her smile quivering. Caro held out a hand and Sasha took it, sitting down suddenly and, without warning, horrifying herself and probably horrifying Caroline too, burst into unstoppable tears.

CHAPTER EIGHT

CAROLINE was wise enough to let her cry herself out, and when Sasha's sobs died away she sat with her hands over her face, wishing she was somewhere else. Caro leaned over and pushed a paper tissue into her fingers.

'Thanks,' Sasha muttered, very flushed. She dried her face and blew her nose and couldn't look at Caro. Instead she stared at the continental quilt, following the delicate pink scrolls of flowers and leaves printed on it.

'Sorry, I don't know why I broke down like that. I just had a pretty edgy session with Jake, and I don't like scenes.' She forced a smile, glancing up at Caro and then away again quickly. 'I was expecting you to be angry, when you were so kind it was too much.'

'You had *another* row with Jake?' Caroline asked, sounding incredulous, and she nodded without answering. 'Jake rarely quarrels with anyone, he's too lazy,' said Caro with a smile audible in her voice.

'Well, he quarrels with me,' Sasha told her bitterly. 'Almost every time we see each other we get into a snarling match, but I doubt if I'll ever set eyes on him again now. I told him some home truths that nearly took his ears off—he was so furious he drove off just now without even saying goodbye!'

Caroline began to laugh, and Sasha looked up

then, incredulous and a little offended. She saw
nothing funny in what she had just said, her sense
of humour was as good as anybody's, but she
could see no humour in this situation. Caro met
her unamused eyes and sobered.

Sasha drew a hurried breath and plunged into a
stammered apology, she had to get it out of the
way; Caroline obviously knew what had happened
earlier when James Fox overheard the scene in the
sitting-room, she must be waiting for an explanation and an apology. 'I'm sorry I jumped to stupid
conclusions about you and Jake—it was inexcus-
able of me, I'm ashamed of myself. I hope I didn't
make too much trouble, didn't make your
husband too angry, I can't tell you how sorry I
am . . .'

Caro interrupted the anxious sentences, leaning
forward to pat her hand and smile at her. 'Don't
be so worried, it was partly my fault.'

'Oh, no!' Sasha protested quickly.

'Oh, yes,' Caro said with wry self-mockery. 'To
tell you the truth, I was a bit jealous.'

Sasha stared at her, mouth parted in a gasp of
dismay. What was Caroline confessing? She did
not want to hear, suddenly; she did not want to sit
there and listen to Caroline Fox talking about
Jake.

'Stupid, I know,' said Caro. 'It isn't easy to
explain how it is with Jake and me—I love him
dearly, always have, and he has always belonged
to me in one way, as much as he ever belonged to
anyone. Jake's a guy who loves his freedom, he
hates to be tied down by anything or anyone. I've
seen it happen dozens of times—he dates someone
for a while, they fall for him and start attaching

strings to him, and Jake runs.'

'He likes it kept light,' Sasha said bitterly. 'I know, you don't have to tell me, I worked him out myself—that's just what I've been telling him today, that he's too selfish and shallow to be worth bothering about.'

Caroline frowned, watching her intently. 'Oh, no—you're wrong! Jake isn't like that at all—on the contrary, I'd say he was afraid of getting too involved because he's scared of getting hurt.' She leaned forward, speaking very seriously. 'Don't you see? How could he act the way he does if he wasn't capable of deep feelings?'

Sasha looked down, her face paling, a sharp little pain stabbing inside her. 'Towards you?' she murmured, and told herself that the bitter resentment she felt was because Caro Fox had no right to gamble with the happiness of her husband and child, she had no right to encourage Jake's love for her.

Caroline sighed. 'He used to think he loved me, but he didn't. He's fond of me, we're fond of each other, but it isn't the sort of love you're talking about. Jake's highly sexed . . .'

Sasha stiffened, the stabbing inside her becoming intolerable. 'I don't want to hear about his sex life,' she muttered, getting up. She had to get away before Caro told her the intimate secrets of her relationship with Jake.

'I couldn't tell you anything you haven't read in the gossip columns,' Caro said, her voice wry. 'Except what I've worked out for myself about him—that Jake has confused sex with love for years. It isn't surprising; his career took off too early, he shot into the limelight before he'd had a chance to get to know himself. When you're a big star overnight and women fight to get a date with you, you'd have to be a very exceptional person to keep your head, to stay modest about yourself.' She laughed, shaking her head. 'Not that Jake was ever what I'd call modest; he was always the guy playing around, he didn't take himself seriously then.'

'He does now,' said Sasha. 'He has too much ego to care a twopenny damn about anyone else.'

'That's what I've been trying to explain—we all learn about life at different rates, depending on what happens to us. Jake was shoved into a hothouse when he was very young; women threw themselves at him, how could he be expected to put any sort of value on what he got so easily? That's why he thought he wanted me, for a while—because I was unattainable. That made me special to him; I was the one who got away. If I'd ever given in and gone to bed with him he would soon have realised how he really felt about me.'

Sasha sat down again, her throat dry. Caroline watched her in silence for a moment, and outside the drowsy birds called in the garden and the shadows lengthened as evening approached.

'I'm not in love with Jake and I never have been,' said Caro, and Sasha started, her eyes wide, as she was broken out of her own thoughts. 'But he's very special to me, we came very close when we were young, and you never quite forget the friends you had when you were young, do you? When you get older you're reluctant to care so much about other people; it's a little like disillusion. As you get older you realise that most people are nowhere near as exciting and mysterious as you once thought they were . . .'

'You said you were jealous of me,' Sasha stammered, flushing a little as Caro smiled wryly.

'Not in the way you think—it's just that I'm possessive about my friends; Jake's a big star, I'm proud of him, I'm happy to know I'm special to him. I suppose I saw you as a threat to our old friendship; you're not like the other women he's dated, I could see you were different. His women are usually . . .'

'I am *not* one of his women!' Sasha broke in angrily.

She was stiff with insulted pride; she wasn't accepting that from Caroline. It would have infuriated her from anyone, but from Caro Fox it was a deadly insult because she was jealous of her. She stared at the window, paling, as she admitted that to herself. It was pointless to be jealous, but she was, she had been from the start. She couldn't help noticing how Jake smiled at Caro, their intimacy had been a thorn under her skin right from the beginning.

'Are you offended?' Caro asked anxiously. 'Please, all I meant was that you're different from the other girls I've seen him with—he treats you as if he cared about you.'

Sasha felt a tremor of feeling run through her; hope, sadness? She wasn't sure which. 'Has he told you how we first met?' she asked, looking at Caro, and saw from her face that Jake had not mentioned Philip's death or his own involvement. What did that tell her about him? Why had he kept it to himself? She began to tell Caro, who listened intently, only saying once with shock: 'My

God!' and then when Sasha had fallen silent, 'I'm sorry, so sorry, how terrible it must have been for you.'

'It doesn't hurt so much any more,' Sasha said, and wasn't sure if she was admitting that to Caro or to herself. 'In a way that's painful too. Some days I hardly think of Philip at all. It makes you wonder how real life is, do you know what I mean? If you can forget someone who once meant so much to you, what does anything matter?'

Caro looked at her in appalled sympathy. 'You mustn't think like that! It's dangerous! A bit like looking down from the top of a skyscraper—you get emotional vertigo. I do know what you mean, of course. I once lost a baby before I had Madeleine. I didn't think I'd ever get over that, but we do. We have to start living again.'

'I have,' Sasha said. 'But I wouldn't want to care that much about someone else. I couldn't go through that sort of experience again.'

Caro looked at her with wry gentleness. 'Lovey, I don't think we're given the choice. I think you're half in love with Jake already.'

Sasha flushed. 'Oh, no! Not Jake Redway! Not me! I'm not that much of a fool, thank you.'

James Fox put his head round the door, his expression quizzical. 'Phone for you, Sasha,' he said, his glance shooting from her to his smiling wife.

She stayed where she was, frowning. 'Who is it?'

He shrugged. 'I'm sorry, I didn't ask.'

'What's the betting it's Jake?' said Caroline, laughing, but James shook his head with a dry little smile, walking into the room and sitting down on the bed.

'It isn't Redway,' he said, and Sasha got up, certain that if it had been Jake, James would have recognised his voice. She went downstairs and picked up the phone.

'Hallo, Sasha Lewis speaking.'

'Sasha, love, how are you?' She recognised her agent's voice without him identifying himself. 'I've been trying to get in touch with you for days, I've only just found out where you are—why didn't you leave your address?'

'I did,' she told him sardonically. His secretary had obviously forgotten all about her visits, probably hadn't even remembered her name.

'Can you audition tomorrow? I've been offered a small part for you, they want you to be there at eleven tomorrow—can you make it?'

'What do you think?' Sasha said, and he laughed.

'That's my girl! Got a pencil?' He gave her some details which she wrote down, then he said coyly: 'What's all this about you and Jake Redway? Is it all rumours or are you . . .'

'Thanks for ringing,' Sasha said, and hung up.

She tapped before she opened Caroline's bedroom door. James was just getting up, a slight flush on his cheekbones. He said coolly: 'Good news, I hope?'

Sasha told them, struggling not to sound too excited, and Caroline's face lit up with sympathetic delight. 'How marvellous—I'm so pleased!' She laughed. 'I'll be sorry to lose you, of course; it's been great fun having you here, you've been wonderful with Madeleine, and I'll miss you, but I do hope you get the part.'

'Even if I do—which is a million to one shot,

there are bound to be dozens of others after it—I wouldn't have to go into rehearsal for ages,' Sasha pointed out.

'I must get back to my briefs,' said James Fox, moving to the door. 'I have half a dozen opinions to give before the end of the month. As it's Friday tomorrow, you might as well stay in London all weekend, Sasha—you're due for some time off.'

When he had gone, Caroline said: 'James is right; if you have any old flames tucked away, now's the time to bring them out—a lighthearted date, that's what you need, some fun and no strings, it will take your mind off Jake.'

'My mind's not on him!'

'It's time Jake learnt a lesson,' said Caro, ignoring that, with a crusading light in her eyes.

'I'll drink to that,' Sasha said bitterly. She would love to teach Jake Redway a lesson about women, but she would only be fooling herself if she imagined she could do it; that thick head of his was impervious, he already thought he knew all there was to know about women. He might be an expert on sex, no doubt he had all the experience in the world in that area, but what he knew about how women really felt could be written on a postage stamp.

The audition was being held at a small theatre just off St Martin's Lane, a short walk from Trafalgar Square. Sasha said goodbye to James Fox as they left the railway station early that morning, and set off to walk, since she had over an hour before she was due at the theatre. The sky was the tender blue of summer mornings before the sun has fully risen, the streets full of hurrying office workers, around Nelson's Column the

pigeons strutted and flapped, and Sasha slowly
walked across the square thinking about Jake
Redway and hoping she would never see him
again. By the time she reached the theatre she had
almost convinced herself she disliked him and
despised his attitudes to everything except his
career. She couldn't fault him on that—she had
never seen him act, but he would not be so
successful if he didn't concentrate intensely on his
work. Maybe that was why he had never really
cared about anyone, if he gave any of that
attention to a woman his work would suffer, he
put so much into acting that there was no feeling
left for other people—except, of course, Caro Fox
and Maggie.

Any woman who let herself care about Jake
Redway would get badly hurt; it had been wise of
Caroline to choose James Fox instead. He might
be somewhat alarming, but he loved her.

She identified herself at the stage door and was
directed down a badly lit, narrow corridor. While
she walked there, she hadn't allowed herself to
think ahead to the audition, but now that she was
at the theatre her hands and feet were icy cold and
her stomach was full of butterflies. Auditions were
always nerve-racking; she tried to relax, pinning a
bright, false smile on her face, as she saw a young
man in a thin red shirt and jeans walking towards
her.

'Hallo,' he said, staring, then looked at the
clipboard in his hand. 'Are you . . .'

'Sasha Lewis,' she said, trying to glimpse the
names on his list and wondering how many others
were being auditioned for the part.

'Right,' he said, offering her his hand and

smiling briefly. 'I'm Don Browning, I'm stage manager here. Will you come along and meet Harley? He's waiting for you.' He turned and hurried off without waiting for an answer, clutching his clipboard and muttering to himself like the White Rabbit. 'No time, never get it all done . . .'

Sasha caught up with him, breathless. 'Did you say Harley? Harley Akin? He's directing the play?'

Don nodded, giving her a strange quick look; as though taken aback by her question. Sasha's stomach knotted in cramp; Harley Akin was a notoriously tough director who worked his actors until they broke up in little pieces, but was nevertheless so brilliant that actors fought to get into his productions. Sasha couldn't believe that he would consider giving her a part, however small, in one of his plays. Why hadn't her agent warned her that Harley was directing? How could he do this to her—throwing her unwarned into an audition which would end up with her staggering away feeling like death?

They emerged on to a bare stage; the curtain up and only the brick walls at the back for scenery. A pale blue light was directed on to the centre of the stage and in it stood two men talking; one of them the bald-headed Harley Akin in a grey track-suit which made him look like a rumpled elephant, and the other a lean man in a black shirt and jeans, who turned his head at the creak of footsteps on the bare boards. Sasha stopped dead as she recognised him, her lips parting in a muffled gasp of shock and anger. What was Jake Redway doing here?

Jake turned to face her, his blue eyes darting

over her pale face, reading her expression with a little quirk of wry amusement. 'You're late,' he said. 'Come and meet Harley.'

Sasha didn't move, she couldn't her feet were apparently growing down into the boards and she felt rage leaping and roaring inside her. Jake had set this up! How dared he play God like this? Why had he done it?

He strolled over and stood in front of her, blocking her from the director's view, staring down at her with narrowed, mocking eyes. 'Don't chuck your chance away. Harley's not a patient man and this is a chance in a million for you. It's only a small part, but with Harley directing it could be the making of you.'

'You asked him to audition me,' she accused in a low stammer, shaking.

'Yes, he wants me to do the play, so for the moment I've got some pull with him, but it won't last once I've signed the contract. One actor in the bush is worth ten in the hand.' He grinned at her, but she did not smile back, she did not think he was funny.

'I don't want the part,' she said through almost closed lips, and he took hold of her arm and hustled her further away, out of earshot of Harley Akin.

'I've gone to a great deal of trouble for you!'

'I didn't ask you to! I'll get my own parts, I won't have you pulling strings for me. What will Mr Akin think?'

Jake stared down at her broodingly; his brows drawn in a black line above those angry blue eyes. 'He thinks you're my latest lady love—what else would he think?'

The unabashed admission made hot colour flow up her face. 'Well, you can disabuse him—I'm nothing of the kind and . . .'

'Who the hell cares? What does it matter what anybody thinks? What's wrong, Sasha? Can't you act? Is that it? You don't think you're good enough for this part? You can't do it? Chickening out?'

The drawled contempt in his voice made her stiffen, her hands curling into fists at her sides. 'Of course I could do it! That's beside the point. If this audition had been above board, if he had wanted me because he'd seen me act, I'd have jumped at the chance, but not like this!'

His hand tightened and he shook her. 'Listen, if Harley doesn't think you can do it, he won't give you the part anyway. I got you the audition—I didn't get you anything but a chance to show Harley what you can do. The rest is up to you.'

She looked at him, silenced, uneasy, doubtful. Jake stared back at her, lifting one eyebrow in question. 'Well?' he insisted when she didn't speak. 'Are you going to read for him or not?'

She thought, her head lowered to avoid his watchful eyes. She wanted the chance to get a part in one of Harley Akin's plays and what did it really matter how she had got this audition? People might whisper, it might get around, but she could ignore the needling little comments, the smiles and sideways looks. Harley's reputation as a director of integrity would silence most of the gossip, and she was under no illusions about how hard she would have to work if she was to satisfy his high standards. Jake was quite right, it was a chance in a million, and she would be a fool if she didn't take the chance he had handed to her on a plate.

'Well?' Jake demanded again, and she looked up, nodding.

'Yes,' she said in a low tone, and his mouth twisted.

'Your gratitude is overwhelming.'

'Thank you,' she said reluctantly, and he looked at her as if he would like to hit her.

'I don't know why I bothered, you waspish little bitch!' He turned and walked back to Harley Akin, and after a moment's hesitation, Sasha followed him. The director gave her a thoughtful, curious stare as he shook hands, then put her through a searching catechism about her experience and views on the theatre. Jake stood listening, his long lean body casually at rest yet disturbing her even though she did not look his way; she was aware of him all the time and angry with herself for being so conscious of him.

'Have you seen the text?' Harley asked a few moments later, and she shook her head. He glanced at Jake, his eyes amused, but only said: 'Then I'll have to give you a quick rundown on the action and the character you'd be playing. She's a minor character but vital to the play.'

Sasha listened to his outline of the story, then he handed her a script and asked her to sit down and study a few pages. Jake moved a chair into the centre of the stage. Harley walked off, and Sasha sat and glanced through the script.

'I'll cue you in,' said Jake, a hand on the back of her chair and his tall body stooping over her, making her breathless with a mixture of sensitivity and anger. 'Like to do a run-through first?'

'No rehearsal,' said Harley from the front row of the stalls, making her jump. 'I want her to do it cold.'

'Is that fair?' Jake started to say, and was cut short.

'You're quite capable of doing a bit of cunning direction,' Harley mocked him. 'I want to get an idea of how *her* mind works, not how yours does.' He leaned back, smiling sarcastically. 'I know all about your mind.'

'Sure you do!' Jake muttered, but shrugged.

Sasha stood up, swallowing; her throat dry and rusty and her skin very cold. 'Ready?' Harley asked, and she nodded. She was as ready as she would ever be, she might as well get it over with, but she knew she would never be able to get any feeling into the little scene, the only emotion she was capable of at the moment was sheer blind terror. Her mind was blank, she moistened her lips and the lines of black words danced up and down in front of her eyes. What did they mean? Why had she ever wanted to go on the stage, anyway? She must be crazy; it was no job for a sane person, it was torture and masochism.

'Okay, that will do,' a voice said somewhere, and she stopped, mouth open and eyes wide, staring down into the dark auditorium. Harley Akin was standing a few feet below her and he smiled at her calmly while she just gazed at him dazedly, only now realising that she had done the scene, that it was over, she must have gone through the lines in a dull trance without being aware of her surroundings.

'Jake, I'd like a word,' Harley said, and Jake vanished, leaving her standing on the bare stage with the script in her hand. She dropped it on the chair and walked slowly into the wings, her legs trembling under her. Somehow she found her way back through the labyrinth of passages to the stage door and out into the summer sunshine. She hadn't got the part, she knew it, there seemed no point in waiting around to hear Harley politely apologising.

She walked across Charing Cross Road into Leicester Square and went into a small café; she badly needed a cup of strong black coffee. The leaves of the trees in the centre of the square, around Shakespeare's statue, whispered and shifted, making soft lacy shadows on the tarmac below. Crowds drifted around the square, and she watched them without really seeing them.

Why had Jake Redway talked Harley into giving her that audition? Well, that was obvious enough; he wanted her in his debt, and she could guess without any difficulty how he would expect her to pay him back for his help. It happened all the time, in their business, in a lot of other businesses; it would be stupid to feel surprised. A lot of girls would see it as a compliment, Jake must want her badly if he was prepared to go to all that trouble to get her. He certainly didn't have to make such an effort with most women; they flung themselves eagerly into his arms. She stirred her cooling coffee, staring into it blankly, remembering the wild intensity she had felt when he kissed her in his car. It frightened her rigid; she didn't want to feel like that, her whole body had seemed to be on fire. Jake was the last man in the world she wanted to get involved with—she knew with aching certainty that he would hurt her, and she couldn't face the pain of falling in love with him.

She made her way to Billy's shop and found him alone, polishing silver at a table at the back. 'Hallo,' he said, looking surprised. 'What are you doing up in London? Date with Jake Redway?' and then he laughed and Sasha glared at him.

'Not funny!'

'No?' Billy regarded her, head to one side. 'Make some coffee, there's a love; Karen and the boys are at the Zoo. The dreaded school holidays are upon us, Karen's going spare trying to think of ways of occupying them.'

Sasha made some coffee and they sat down at the table. Sasha polished with him, it was an endless task, like painting the Forth Bridge, you had no sooner finished than you had to start again.

'So what's all this about Jake Redway?' Billy asked. 'Karen's opened a cuttings book—three pieces so far, she's getting quite excited.'

'She needn't bother; there's nothing in it.' Sasha polished energetically; she needed to do something with all her anger and resentment. Billy leaned back and watched her thoughtfully, his spectacles on the end of his nose; he still looked Byronic when he wasn't smiling, it was an odd fluke of fate that favoured him with such hauntingly poetic looks when he was by nature a very quiet, ordinary man.

'Odd that he was the guy who pulled you out of the sea,' he observed, and she nodded.

'One of those weird coincidences,' she muttered, polishing harder than ever.

'I wish you wouldn't keep everything to yourself so much,' Billy said plaintively. 'You're so secretive. We're your family, we care about you—I sometimes think you would rather have been an orphan, I suppose that's the artistic temperament we hear so much about—we're not romantic enough for you!' He was teasing her, she looked up and he smiled over his glasses, but she felt guilty, which was probably what he had intended. It was a form of emotional blackmail; love always was, whatever its complexion. When someone said they cared about you they were also demanding that you care about them. There was no such thing as a unilateral declaration of love—it was always a bartered emotion; if I give to you will you give to me? Love was always selfish, from the cradle upwards people clamoured to be loved and if they did not get they rarely gave. Even when they seemed to love without hope of a return they were getting something out of it, even if it was only a masochistic pleasure in the pain of hopeless loving.

Sasha loved her brother; she looked at him wryly and shrugged. 'I've seen Jake Redway a few times, that's all—big deal, I have plenty of competition, he's no celibate. I'm not going to make a song and dance about having a couple of dates with the man, I leave that to the press. I said: there's nothing to tell.'

'Why do I get the feeling you're protesting too much?' Billy enquired.

'I'm telling you the truth,' Sasha said flatly. 'I haven't been to bed with him . . .'

'I didn't suggest you had!' Billy jumped in, frowning.

'I doubt if I'll see him again, in fact,' said Sasha, her mouth turning down at the edges in spite of her attempts to stop it.

Billy said: 'I see,' in a voice she found galling,

and stared at her so hard that she flushed to her hairline.

'I'm not in love with him!' she muttered furiously, scarlet. 'I wish people would stop trying to prove I am.' She wished a lot more than that: she wished Jake Redway had never come back into her life, she wished he would vanish off the face of the earth, she wished she could think of some way of showing him she didn't care twopence about him, it would give her a hell of a lot of satisfaction to make him see what a selfish swine he was.

'You *are* in a tizzy,' Billy said with brotherly compassion. 'We'll have to think of something to cheer you up—why don't we all have dinner out tonight? When Karen gets back she can fix up a babysitter and we'll get dressed up and go out in style.' He smiled with pleasure at his idea. 'We haven't been out for ages; it will be fun.'

Sasha did not feel like having dinner out, she felt like hibernating somewhere quiet and peaceful, but she looked at her brother's happy smile and held her tongue.

'Okay?' Billy asked without a shred of doubt that she would jump at the offer, and Sasha said simply: 'Thank you, that would be great.'

It didn't quite work out like that. When Karen got back at five o'clock she was yawning and flushed, exhausted by a day spent in Regents Park with the two boys. They were flaked out, too; they wearily kissed Sasha and had some milk and a boiled egg and toast, then trailed off to bed, too tired even to squabble the way they normally did over the two teddy bears who also occupied their bedroom, and whose possession was heatedly disputed each evening. The largest was the most cherished, Sasha had given him to Alex when he was two as a consolation for the arrival of his new brother; both boys wanted him, but tonight they just climbed into bed and fell asleep without caring whose bed he was sitting on.

'I'm sorry, I couldn't go out again,' said Karen, slumping into a chair in front of the TV. 'You two go, though, I'm not fit to move a muscle anyway. I'll be quite happy in front of the TV and I'm going to bed early.'

'No, it doesn't matter,' Sasha said, but Billy said firmly: 'Oh yes, it does; we're going out. You need a change of scene and so do I. Anyway, I've booked a table now.'

'I'm not dressed for dinner anywhere special,' Sasha protested, looking down at the blue cotton pants and matching loose tunic top she wore.

'I'll drive you home and you can change,' Billy informed her, disposing of that argument, and Karen smiled at her sleepily.

'Don't argue, just let him have his own way, it makes him happy.'

Billy made a face at her. 'If there's one thing I hate, it's being *managed*! You make me feel I'm one of the boys.'

'So you are,' said Karen, yawning, a hand flapping over her mouth. 'Oh, I'm so tired, my feet are throbbing and I could sleep for a hundred years!' She smiled at Sasha. 'Next time I have a bright idea about going to the Zoo I'll stick them in front of the telly instead!'

Billy drove Sasha over to her flat and while she was changing he sat down to watch a programme on TV. She had taken most of her clothes down to the Fox house, she frowned gloomily over her

limited wardrobe, and decided the only possible
dress she could wear was the blue silk dress she
had bought for the last night party of her play.
While she was doing her face a few moments later
the phone rang and Billy answered it. He tapped
on her bedroom door a second later and said with
a grin: 'Guess who?'

To her fury Sasha felt herself go pink. Billy
laughed and she muttered: 'I've no idea, I don't
have my crystal ball with me.'

'Come off it,' said Billy. 'Go on—he's in a
pretty impatient mood, from the sound of his
voice.'

Sasha reluctantly walked past him and picked
up the phone. 'Hallo, who's speaking?'

'Who was that?' Jake asked without replying to
her question.

'What?' She was confused for a second, aware of
Billy hovering around, listening.

'The guy who answered the phone,' Jake said
impatiently. 'Who was it? Why did he laugh when
I told him my name?'

'I'm just going out to dinner, I haven't got time
to talk now,' Sasha said without answering the
questions.

'With him? Who is it?' Jake asked, then without
waiting for an answer said: 'Don't you want to
hear how you did at the audition?'

'I know how I did—I was hopeless,' she said
bitterly because she was angry with him for having
got her into the audition in the first place. 'I must
go, my date is waiting.'

'I want to talk to you. Do you hear me, Sasha?'
Jake snarled, abandoning any pretence of being
polite. 'You got the part, you idiot.'

Her hand gripped the phone, she stiffened. 'That isn't funny!'

'You got it!' Jake told her. 'Harley liked you, he was quite impressed.'

Sasha's stomach was heaving; she felt sick and dizzy and feverish and she couldn't believe what he was saying. Her hand shook so much she put the phone down without a word, and Billy looked at her with surprise and curiosity.

'Something wrong, Sasha? What was all that about?'

'He must have been lying; it can't be true,' she said. Or if Jake had been telling the truth, and Harley had given her that part, it couldn't have been because of her own ability. She knew she had put up an abysmal performance, she had gone totally blank and wooden, she couldn't remember a word she had said or an action she had performed. If Harley had given her that part it must be because Jake had insisted on it, and if Jake had insisted on it, she knew what he would expect to get from her in return.

'Oh, no!' she exclaimed, grabbing her jacket. 'Not me, he isn't getting me!'

'I wish I knew what you were talking about,' Billy complained, following her out of the flat. 'Why are you running? What's after us? Or can I guess?'

Billy's car didn't start first time, and he muttered and grumbled as he pulled the choke out 'Weather like this and it needs some choke— ridiculous! I'm going to get a new car.'

Sasha was watching as a vehicle turned the corner of the road; her whole body tense as she recognised it. Billy's engine burst into life at last and he moved off slowly, back in a good humour again.

'Okay, problem over,' he told her, turning to smile at her, and saw her face. 'Hey, don't look like that!' he exclaimed, and put an arm round her to hug her, swerving slightly as the other car passed them. Sasha avoided the eye of the driver and the angry blare of his horn. Billy made a rude gesture at him out of the window, and laughed at her. 'Does he think he owns the road? Noisy swine!'

As they turned out of the road Sasha looked back and saw the other car swing round in the road and follow them. Billy sped off and took a short cut through some back streets. Sasha kept her eye on the road behind them. There was no sign of anyone on their tail, they had shaken him off. She heaved a sigh of relief; thank heavens Billy hadn't recognised him, it would have been so embarrassing to have to ask her brother to take evasive action to lose Jake Redway's car, Billy would have pulled her leg unmercifully.

A quarter of an hour later they parked and went into the restaurant where Billy had booked. Sasha wasn't hungry, but Billy was enjoying himself so much that she forced herself to relax and at least pretend to be enjoying the meal.

'We ought to do this more often,' Billy decided several hours later as he paid the bill before they left. 'All of us—Karen should get out more than she does, next time we'll all go.'

'You ought to take Karen out, just the two of you,' Sasha told him. 'That would be a much better idea. Why not have tomorrow together? I'll stay and mind the shop and the boys. It would do Karen good, she looked wiped out tonight.'

Billy wasn't hard to persuade, he let himself be talked into it without putting up much of a struggle, and Sasha went back with him to spend the night in the spare room so that he and Karen could make an early start next day. Being Billy he had decided to kill two birds with one stone—he was going to drive up to Cambridge to an auction being held next day, he might buy some nice silver and he could given Karen a day's holiday at the same time, he said happily.

Sasha spent the day working in the shop and keeping an eye on the two boys; which wasn't easy, they were as lively as a jar of spilt marbles, she couldn't imagine how Karen's nerves could stand it. At their excited request she made the boys beefburgers and chips for lunch, with a double helping of chocolate icecream to follow. She let the lunch drag out because at least while they were sitting at the table eating she knew what they were up to and could relax a little.

Billy and Karen got back at seven and Sasha had dinner with them; she had prepared a colourful salad and had sliced ham and chicken in advance. When they had eaten and been in to kiss the two sleeping boys Sasha sat talking to them for an hour before she looked at her watch, yawning. 'I'm off,' she said.

'Thanks for taking over today,' Karen told her 'We had a lovely day, I hope you aren't too exhausted.'

'It was fun,' Sasha assured her. 'I enjoyed it, I hope the boys did.'

'I'll drive you back,' said Billy, wandering

towards the door, and Sasha waved a hand at her sister-in-law and followed him.

By the time she reached her flat it was half past ten. She met Mrs Hughes in the hall, letting out her cats. Sasha had to stop for a chat and Mrs Hughes said curiously: 'Your phone hasn't stopped ringing all day. If I'd had a key I could have let myself in and answered it, it might have been urgent.'

'I doubt it,' said Sasha, feeling very disturbed. She looked at her watch and said she must get some sleep, she was dead. Mrs Hughes stood in the hall watching her climb the stairs. The phone was ringing as Sasha let herself into the flat, but it stopped before she could pick it up. She wasn't sure whether she was relieved about that or disappointed.

She had a quick bath and got into bed in a short cotton nightie, feeling like the survivor of a long and gruelling battle; children were energy-consuming. She put out the light after reading for a few minutes and almost at once fell asleep.

She dreamt she was on a cruise liner in the middle of a vast ocean and there was a fire alarm, she heard bells ringing and people shouting, but there was so much smoke she couldn't see where to go. She dragged herself, breathless with urgency, up towards the night air and the deck, and then realised she was awake and there *were* bells; the telephone was ringing again. There was some smoke too, of a sort; a pale moonlight swirled through the room, giving a strange air to the familiar surroundings.

Fumbling for the clock, she dropped it and it rolled across the room. The alarm went off and it rang in unison with the shrilling telephone. Sasha ran after it, stumbling; she switched the alarm off and then groped for the phone.

'Hallo?' she asked irritably.

'Where were you all last night?' a harsh voice demanded, and she snapped wide awake in one second flat.

She looked at the clock she held. 'It's midnight,' she said in disbelief.

'You weren't at Caro's,' Jake snarled. 'Where the hell did you get to, and who was that guy you went off with? You told me there hadn't been anyone else since your husband died! What was *he*, a mirage?'

Sasha shook the clock as though believing it was telling the wrong time. 'You woke me up,' she said. 'It's the middle of the bloody night, are you crazy? Go to sleep and leave me alone!'

'Tell me first . . .' Jake began, and she yelled into the phone.

'Shove off!' She slammed it down and dropped the alarm clock into her waste paper basket. It could ring there. She was about to get into bed again when the phone started to ring. Sasha went over, picked it up, put it down on the table and on an afterthought covered it with a teacosy and two cushions. Then she crawled back into bed and fell straight back into sleep.

CHAPTER NINE

SHE was still in bed next morning when someone banged on the front door of the flat. Sasha sat up, hesitating between ignoring the noise and opening the door with the chain firmly barring entry. In the end she slid out of bed, put on a thin cotton wrap and went over to open the door. Jake glared through the narrow opening.

'Let me in, I want to talk to you.'

'No, go away,' Sasha said. He was in black pants and a tight-fitting black shirt; he looked casual and dangerous all at the same time, and she did not want him near her. It wasn't so much that she didn't trust him—which, of course, she didn't, not an inch—as that she didn't trust herself. She found the sight of him far too damned pleasant.

'I don't understand you,' Jake accused, inserting a foot into the space between door frame and door. 'Don't you want that part?'

'I'm not auditioning in bed,' Sasha informed him, and his eyes darkened to a savage glare. Bad temper only made him better-looking, she thought irrelevantly.

'Charming! Did I ask you to? So that's what you think, is it?'

'That's what I think,' she said. 'And if you don't take your foot out of my door I'll cripple you for life!'

'Will you open this door and let me in?' he yelled with a ferocity which made her jump, then suddenly withdrew his foot. Surprised, she stared through the gap at him as he took several steps away. She should have taken the chance to shut the door. She didn't, because as he seemed about to walk away she felt her heart take a nose-dive and she stupidly did not want him to go. It was a full moment before she understood his intentions. He charged the door at top speed and with a yelp of alarm she leapt out of the way as he crashed into the panels. The chain broke and the door swung open. Jake came through and closed it, leaning against it with a self-satisfied grin.

Sasha was speechless for a few seconds, then her temper flared. 'How dare you break my door? You're crazy—I should call the police!'

'Shut up,' Jake muttered, breathing rapidly after such violent exertion. He fingered his left shoulder, grimacing. 'I think I've bruised the bone.'

'Serves you right, a pity you didn't break a few,' Sasha said bitterly. 'If you've come to collect for getting me that part you can forget it—I don't want the part that badly.'

'I ought to slap you,' Jake said hoarsely, straightening and moving towards her. 'That's a deadly insult, or don't you know anything about men? Do you think I have to use that sort of ploy to get a woman?'

'Oh, of course, you only have to whistle and they drop down out of the trees, don't you? I suppose you thought *I'd* be that easy, you've tried to get me into bed a couple of times now and failed, so you came up with the idea of putting me under an obligation.'

'Tried?' Jake repeated, staring down at her with narrowing eyes, and she felt suddenly very nervous under the expression in that stare. 'Oh, no, Sasha, I haven't even begun to try yet; when I turn on the heat you'll really know all about it!' His hands shot out before she could back, his fingers digging into her shoulders and making her wince.

'Harley gave you that part without any pressure from me—I just talked him into seeing you—I know him too well to try to influence his actual decision. If I'd tried I'd have pushed him in the opposite direction; he's as obstinate as a pig. You did very well at the audition; I'd told him you were good, and you proved it.'

She frowned, her eyes lifting to his face, searching it uncertainly for some sign as to whether he was telling the truth. 'I don't remember doing the scene,' she admitted huskily. 'I blanked out. I thought I'd made a fool of myself.'

He smiled gently and she blinked in surprise at the warmth in his blue eyes. 'You didn't, I promise you. It isn't a big part, but you've got it if you want it. We go into rehearsals in six weeks' time. It's a limited run, opening out of London and then doing maybe three months in the West End, if we're lucky.' His voice became mocking. 'If you can stand being in the same theatre with me for that long!'

Sasha fixed her nervous eyes on the brown throat which was just on a level with her head; his shirt collar was open, he wasn't wearing a tie. She felt him watching her and was anxiously aware of the fact that she herself was only wearing a very thin silk nightdress under the wrap, the belt of which had come undone so that the lapels of the wrap had drifted apart leaving Jake an unobscured view of her high, rounded breasts with their hard, pink nipples showing through the silk. A slow tremor of aroused passion passed through her, her skin began to burn, and she heard Jake draw a fierce breath.

'You're beautiful,' he whispered, and one hand slid down her arm and moved inside the wrap to touch the warm soft flesh under the silk. 'You can't blame me for wanting you; you're irresistible, Sasha!'

She hated the smile in his voice, the mocking look in the blue eyes. Fury burst out in her and she knocked his hand away. 'Games! That's all it means to you! You treat everything lightly!'

'If I play it light it's because I find it hard to play it any other way.' His voice was low and unsteady, his cheekbones carried a hard dark flush. 'Where were you on Friday night? I sat in my car outside your flat, waiting for you to come back, and you didn't show up. I kept looking at my watch and wondering—it was the worst night of my life, I kept going over the things that could have happened to you. I rang Caro and you hadn't gone back there, I rang Maggie, God knows why, she was asleep and she thought I'd gone crazy, I expect. I rang the police . . .'

'The police?' echoed Sasha, staggered.

'I thought you might have had an accident.' He wasn't looking at her, he was fidgeting, his head lowered, very red. 'You could have crashed, could have been in hospital—anything could have happened. The police thought I was screwy, too— they were polite, they humoured me, but they said that if there had been an accident the next of kin would have been informed, and I didn't have a clue who your next of kin were.'

'You're mad,' Sasha said slowly, and his mouth twisted.

'I came back to the other alternative, then—that you were spending the night with that guy you drove off with.' He swallowed. 'I hated that idea too.'

Sasha was silent, watching him and feeling a sharp little dart of emotion halfway between pain and pleasure. Jake had been jealous; he was admitting it, it must mean that he cared for her—you aren't jealous of someone who means nothing to you. He looked up suddenly and their eyes met and he read the expression in hers with a dark scowl.

'Oh, you like that? Was that why you did it? Caro told me it was time I learnt a few hard lessons—were you teaching me something, Sasha? My God, women are ruthless!'

'Your conceit is unbelievable!' Sasha stammered, fuming. 'I wasn't trying to teach you anything! I was living my own life, doing what I wanted to do, and what you might think about it was neither here nor there. It never even entered my head that you would sit outside my flat all night—why on earth would any sane man do a thing like that?'

'God knows,' he said grimly. 'I ought to see the shrink first thing on Monday morning.'

'Well, you said it,' Sasha told him.

He looked at her quickly, his face flushed and unsure, not quite under control; mouth crooked, eyes almost feverishly bright. 'Sasha,' he said, and put his hand on her waist. 'Sasha, I did a lot of thinking while I sat there all night. I've never sat stone cold sober in a car for hours before, it's amazing what goes through your head when there's nothing to distract you. I kept thinking how I'd feel if you'd been killed or if you'd gone off with some other man. It drove me crazy—I couldn't bear the idea of losing you.'

'I'm not yours to lose,' Sasha flung at him, and he flinched, frowning.

'That was another thing I faced,' he said harshly. 'I told myself you weren't mine, but I couldn't seem to believe it.'

'You'd better start trying harder, then, because I'm not yours—I'm not anybody's but my own.'

'I think I'm in love with you,' Jake said, and she stared into the dark blue eyes and felt dizzy at the intensity of their gaze.

She swallowed hard. 'You *think* you are,' she said slowly. Her mouth trembled. 'You're not sure?' She managed to make the question derisive, but it cost her quite a lot. Jake had moved halfway to meet her, she knew she wanted desperately to run to meet him, but she wouldn't; not now, it was too soon. He still had a lot to learn.

Jake gave a half-angry shrug. 'Sure? No, I'm not sure, because I don't know if the way I feel now is going to last. I'm not even certain I know what love is; the labels I used to tie on it don't seem to fit any more.' He stared at her mouth, then his eyes moved on down over her and she tensed at the open desire in that stare. 'I want you—I used to think that was good enough to qualify as love. I like being with you, I want to see you all the time, there's so much I want to know about you. I've never been so curious about anyone before. You're a mystery, you don't seem to think like other women; your mind is as convoluted as a sea-shell—I keep getting whispers and echoes of what's going on in it but I can never be quite sure I've heard properly, and I'd give anything to know.' He laughed grimly. 'I'm obsessed with you—I think I started being obsessed that night at the party when you called me a third-rate Casanova. I was angry enough to hit you, especially when everybody grinned. But I woke up next morning and found myself thinking about you. I've been thinking about you ever since.'

'And if I went to bed with you I'd stop being a mysterious unknown creature, and turn back into another girl on your list,' Sasha said drily.

Jake said quickly: 'No.'

She smiled at him with cool irony. 'Before you start working me out, I'd have a shot at working yourself out, Mr Redway.' He stared at her and she saw the impatient frustration in his eyes, the waiting tension of a desire she had no intention of satisfying.

'Who was the fellow in the clapped-out old tin can?' Jake demanded brusquely. 'Your boy-friend?'

'My brother!' Sasha admitted, and Jake's mouth opened, but not a sound escaped from it. She couldn't help laughing at his stunned expression and the blue eyes glared at her.

'Your brother? Why are you laughing? Are you being funny?'

'No, it really was my brother—the only thing that's funny is your face!'

'Don't laugh at me, damn you! Why didn't you tell me before—if it really was just your brother?'

'Why should I? You were having so much fun.'

'You mean you were,' Jake muttered, his eyes a very dark, angry blue, and Sasha backed, pulling her wrap closer around her and tying the belt firmly.

'I haven't had any breakfast yet—I'm going to make some coffee, want some?' She moved into the kitchen and Jake prowled around the sitting-room, just a few yards away from her. She heard him pulling books out of her shelves, flicking over pages.

'How big a family do you have?' he asked over his shoulder.

'Just one brother, and my parents, of course. What about you?'

'I'm an only child,' Jake said. 'Parents dead; I'm all alone in the world.' He used that deep, dark brown voice which sent shivers down her back, and Sasha made a wry face at him.

'You're acting,' she accused, and saw his mouth curl upwards in amusement.

'I'm glad you know the difference,' he said ambiguously, and as she carried the jar of coffee from the cupboard to the waiting mugs she thought about that and wondered what he had meant. She waited for the kettle to boil, then became aware of the fact that Jake was very quiet. For a second, she wondered if he had actually gone without saying anything, or if he had gone into the bedroom.

Hurriedly she turned and bumped straight into him. Jake steadied her, his hands on her waist, and she looked up, startled, to find him staring down at her with darkened eyes.

'Sasha,' he groaned, and her heart somersaulted violently, leaving her breathless and trembling. Jake's hands tightened on her waist, pulling her closer, his head came down and their mouths met without Sasha being aware of having stood on tiptoe to meet his lips. Her arms went round his neck, she kissed him back feverishly and with a passion which she couldn't disguise. The silent flat swam round her as she clung, eyes closed, meeting Jake's hunger with her own and forgetting everything but the unleashed need she had been trying so hard to force out of sight.

'I love you, I love you,' he said, and kissed her again, their bodies melting into each other. Sasha swayed backwards, shuddering with aroused excitement, and knocked over a neat pyramid of saucepans; they clattered and crashed across the room, and Jake and Sasha broke apart, eyes wide with shock at the noise.

'God, I wondered what the hell that was,' said Jake, starting to laugh. 'My ears were already ringing so much I thought my blood pressure had shot right through the roof of my skull!'

Sasha was shaking, she put both hands to her hot face. Jake stared down into her dilated eyes then said very softly: 'I love you.'

She didn't know if she believed him or not, she only knew she was sick with passion and she needed to be in his arms, even if he was going to hurt her and leave her one day, even if he didn't mean a word of what he was saying. Her calm resolve had faded into the distance, her self-control was shot to pieces, one touch of his mouth and she was disintegrating.

'Don't hide from me,' he said, taking her wrists and pulling down her hands so that he could see her face. 'Listen, Sasha, I mean it—don't look at me as though you thought I should be certified! When I was sitting in my car outside your flat that night I kept telling myself I was crazy; I can't remember ever doing such a stupid thing before, I was acting like some lovesick schoolboy, but I couldn't go home and not know where you were. I kept wondering: where is she? Who's with her? What's she doing? My head was buzzing with questions. Then I realised I was jealous, I was so jealous I wanted to hit somebody.' He made a wry face, his mouth crooked. 'I couldn't believe it myself, I've never felt that way before.'

'Except about Caroline,' she said quietly.

Jake looked at her with uncertainty. 'I was hopping mad when she married Fox, it's true, but that wasn't how I felt about you. I felt ill; I could feel every nerve in my whole body—they were red-hot, I couldn't sit still. I couldn't bear the way I felt. I wanted to find you; I had to talk to you, but I wasn't even sure what I wanted to say.' He gave her a strange look, his blue eyes puzzled. 'I'm always thinking of things I must say to you, but when you're there I never seem to remember what they were.'

'What sort of things?' Sasha asked curiously, wondering if the questions he wanted to ask her were the same as those she wanted to ask him: what he ate for breakfast, which books he liked most, what music he played when he was alone. She had wanted to ask him a hundred things lately, but she never had; they were always questions she longed to have answered but knew she could never ask.

'I don't know,' he said in restless impatience. 'I don't know anything any more. I miss you when you're not there, I feel empty, as though part of me was missing, I'm hollow, it's frightening. I've never felt I needed anyone before—I don't like it. I don't even know when I started to feel like that. One day you were just a pretty girl I fancied and was curious about; the next I was going around with nothing on my mind but how soon I could see you again. It happened so suddenly, I wasn't expecting to be hit by anything like this.'

'And when you get bored with me? What then, Jake?'

His face shifted in confusion; the blue eyes half angry, half bewildered. 'Are you asking me to guess how I'll feel next year, or the year after? How do I know? I haven't got second sight! I could get knocked down crossing a street tomorrow, or I could live to be a hundred. Who knows? I can't tell you if I'll love you when we're both eighty-three. I would never have prophesied that I'd fall in love with you at all. I only know I'm in love with you now—nothing else seems to matter.'

He released one of her hands and put his fingers lightly on her lips; stroking them until they parted. His eyes held an intensity she had never expected to see in them; it took her breath away.

'You've been in love before,' he said huskily. 'I haven't—not like this. I realise you still haven't got over your husband.' He stopped speaking and she saw him swallow, his eyes dark, as though he was in pain. 'Maybe you never will,' he said, and then she realised that he was jealous of Philip's memory; his mouth was not quite steady.

'I was a different person,' Sasha told him. 'I was only twenty, I didn't know it then, but I was still half a child. My parents were probably wise when they refused to let me marry at eighteen; I wasn't ready for it. I thought I was, of course; I was blazingly angry, I resented having to wait, and after Philip died I think I almost hated my parents for the years I'd lost, the years I could have been with him. But Philip was very calm about waiting; at the time I didn't understand how he could be so calm, but looking back I realise he knew I wasn't old enough, too, he agreed with my parents. He never told me so; Philip was too tactful, and he didn't always tell me what he was thinking.'

Jake was listening intently, watching her changing expressions. She smiled at him.

'It all seems so long ago, I feel as if it had happened to someone else. I can see it much clearer now. I've grown up. Philip's death made me grow up, fast and hard. After that I was never the same. At the time I thought my feelings were deep, but they were only passionate—it isn't the same thing. I loved Philip without knowing him. He was my opposite; I was moody and emotional and Philip was calm and steady. That was what I needed from him, that's why I loved him, but now, you see, I'm such a different person. I've had to learn how to control my feelings, how to control myself. Acting helped. You know how they teach you in drama school to break yourself down, get rid of all your false ideas about yourself, and then start building yourself up again with a much clearer idea of what sort of person you really are . . . well, Philip's death did that for me, even though I tried to duck out on the process. I fought it all the way, I didn't have it easy, and until you made me look hard at the past and at myself, I didn't even know how much I'd learnt, how much I'd changed.'

'You don't still hate me because I didn't save him?' Jake asked in a low voice, his eyes fixed on her face, and Sasha shook her head, her eyes apologetic.

'No, I don't think I ever really hated you, I blamed you because it was easier than blaming myself, but it was Philip's character that caused that accident. He was stubborn; he insisted on going sailing and he didn't check the weather first.'

'Even if I'd heard what you were shouting, I might not have got to him in time,' Jake said heavily.

'I know, I turned on you irrationally. I couldn't help it, you were just a convenient scapegoat. You'd saved my life. I behaved very badly.'

'You were too upset to think straight.'

She laughed wryly. 'At that age, I don't think I ever did think straight! I only knew what I felt, and that's a dangerous way to live.'

'Even more dangerous without feelings,' said Jake, his dark blue eyes full of light and amusement. 'Isn't that what you've been telling me?'

She laughed and he brushed his fingertips along her cheek, making her shiver with response.

'If we're going to be working together for months I'm not going to be able to keep my hands off you,' he murmured, staring at her mouth. 'You've got to start putting the past behind you, Sasha; you can't live alone for ever.'

'I don't intend to,' she said, and he looked sharply at her.

'Is there someone else, then?'

'No,' she said, and smiled up at him.

Jake's mouth twisted. 'I've got a horrible suspicion that you're a tease.'

'I've just learnt to be cautious,' Sasha said. 'If I was sure you really cared about me . . .'

'What do I have to do to make you believe it?' he demanded roughly. 'I've been honest with you—you told me you knew when I was acting. Can't you tell when I'm being honest too? You've had years to get over your first husband . . .'

'I am over him,' she said soberly, and Jake took a fierce breath. Sasha sighed, half smiling. 'And you're right; love can't be guaranteed for ever. I loved Philip when I was twenty, but his memory has faded, I have to look at photographs of him to be certain what he looked like. I realised that the other day; I saw a picture of him at my brother's and had quite a shock. It was like looking at a stranger. It was our wedding photo, and I looked like a stranger, too. That was when I realised how much I'd altered, how long ago I lost Philip.'

Jake pulled her into his arms and kissed her hungrily. She resisted for a second before her body yielded as his hands explored with seductive sensitivity. One touched her breasts; his fingers softly slipping under the thin silk and lace half covering them to caress her warm flesh. His other hand was running down her back, gripping her possessively.

As the sensual insistence of the kiss deepened her arms went helplessly round his neck; she curved closer, her mouth as passionate as his own now, demanding and giving back a mounting desire. Her fingers ran into his hair, winding among the warm strands, she twisted restlessly against him, wanting far more than the tantalising brush of those exploring hands. Deep inside her body she felt an ache of need. When he lifted his head to look at her through his lashes, breathing rapidly, she buried her face on his neck, kissing his brown skin with parted, moist lips. 'Jake, Jake,' she moaned huskily, and felt a hard, fast pulse beating in his throat.

'Love me, Sasha,' he said in a voice so deep it made her nerves leap wildly. She couldn't doubt his emotions at that second; he lifted her chin to look into her face and his eyes burned with passion, she saw the self-abandonment in them as he threw his pride away to show her how much he needed her; Jake was giving helplessly, and no longer demanding a response, simply begging for one. 'I need you—love me,' he whispered, suddenly pale. 'Please love me, Sasha.'

She framed his face with her hands, leaning trustingly against him and feeling the hammering of his heart as her body pressed against his. 'I love you,' she said shakily, and nothing had been so hard to say or meant so much in her life before.

She heard him take a long, deep breath, felt a tremor run through him. 'Sasha,' he said, on a thread of sound, and then didn't say anything else, just looked at her with all that he wasn't saying in his eyes.

'I'm yours,' Sasha said in answer to that look, and he kissed her, holding her so tightly she could scarcely breath. After a few moments she lifted her head, eyes half closed. 'Let's go to bed,' she said breathlessly and with a curling smile, as he opened his eyes in surprise.

'Carry me,' he said, half laughing, half astonished. 'I can't walk, my knees just went.'

'If you can't get there on your own two feet don't bother to come,' Sasha smiled, and walked across the room into the bedroom. Jake was right behind her as she sat down on the bed. He closed the door.

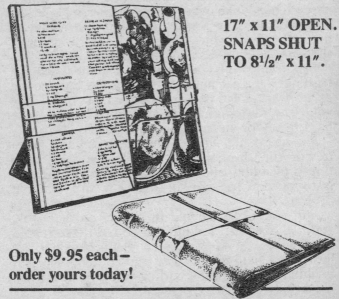